INDIFFERENTS

Casey Giles

Casey Giles
2019

For my family (that includes you, Boodle).

Table of Contents

Chapter I

Broken City

My worn leather boots smack down on the flat roof of a building. I stumble, my knees almost buckling from the fall, but I manage to keep running. It's getting dark. Fast. And bad things happen to those all alone in the dark. Little puffs of white form where I breathe out of my mouth. My back aches, but I'm determined to get to camp as fast as possible. I heft my heavy bag onto my shoulder and peer over the ledge to the next building—it isn't too far down, just a few feet lower.

The wind whistles past my hair and nips at my ears as I jump. Now I really wish I had a hat. My dark, tangled hair is short, but compared to the other boys', it's pretty long. It still doesn't warm up my freezing neck.

It's supposed to be summer, according to the adults back at camp, but you'd never guess it. A gray cloud hangs over the broken city, destroyed again a few days ago by one of the Evils' teams. The city was never exactly beautiful, but ever since, it's taken on a darker undertone. It's been abandoned since we got here—probably for years before then—with weathered and cracked streets, and rust and grime covering the buildings. Rumor has it that they demolished what was left of the city because a Good team was hiding out here. Others say it's because they were searching for something. But what would they need?

I almost trip over our secret hatch while lost in thought. Our building is eight stories tall, with thin walls that allow for lots of corridors, stairs, and rooms. I pull open the little trapdoor and squeeze through, and my feet hit the top rung of the ladder. I'm small for a thirteen-year-old, which makes me a good Scavenger—somebody who finds food and supplies, and can fit through small spaces.

"Jackie!" squeals a little voice.

I stumble down the railing in surprise, sort of half-flipping, half-tumbling. I look up to see my little brother. Nico, short for Nicholas, stares up at me with his big green eyes, a wide smile on his lips.

"Jackie" is one of my many carefully thought-up nicknames that include "Jax," "Scruffy," "Jack-of-all-trades," the infamous (though rarely used) "Jackalope," or just plain old "Jack Barret."

My name is pretty simple, which is why he gives me all of these other sobriquets. So I can be unique, or whatever.

I ruffle Nico's hair. Nicholas and I look so different from each other, people rarely guess that we're only a few years apart. Nico is pale with dark ginger hair, emerald eyes, and a strong build. I, on the other hand, have an olive complexion with a splash of light freckles, dark-chocolate hair, hazel eyes that turn goldish-green, and a small frame. Luckily, I'm still taller than my eight-year-old brother. But lately, he seems to be growing a centimeter a day.

"What'd you find this time, Jax?" he asks, bouncing on the balls of his feet.

I pull out a piece of silk that I salvaged from an empty house. His eyes widen at the shimmering fabric, and he holds out his hands to touch it. It's a pretty rare find. We've been here for about eight years, so there's not much left worth taking. I've heard whispers that the leaders of the camp are considering the idea of moving.

"'S for you," I mumble.

Nico takes the silk and rubs it on his cheek.

"It's *so* soft!" he whispers. "Let's show the Captain!"

Nico makes a *come* gesture, and I follow him into the series of tunnels we use to protect ourselves from invaders. We regularly redirect the hallways and tunnels and relocate several rooms to make it like a maze, so that if someone ever joins a side or leaves without a mission, they won't be able to come back and infiltrate the camp. Whenever Nico doesn't wait for me at the trapdoor, he leaves secret notes in darker parts of the corridors that point to a specific location. No one else knows about this. It's the only secret I keep.

The tunnels are dim, lit up by strings of lights on the walls. Noise travels easily, making the tunnels buzz with conversation. Some corridors slope down into other levels, others have stairs. Nico is a Labyrinth Keeper, meaning that he memorizes and navigates the camp's entryways, exit points, tunnels, and rooms. He's perfect for his job, too, because of his ability: Memory. His skills allow him to remember anything he has witnessed.

Everyone born in our camp has a supernatural ability. Some are extremely beneficial, while others are sort of useless. Many theories float about why we have them, but none have been proven. Some speculate it's an adaptation, and others believe it's caused by chemicals and radiation. I'm not a scientist, so none of this stuff makes any sense to me.

My ability has been named MindSpeak. Without using my voice, I can communicate *to* and *with* others along a two-way telepathic thread, but only people who know me can use the thread, and only if I keep it open. It's rare in terms of known abilities. I'm the only one with MindSpeak in the entire history of the camp. I can also broadcast my thoughts if I'm not paying attention or if I'm nervous, which isn't always ideal. Like if I'm thinking about, say, using the bathroom or whatever, the entire camp may know about my urgent thoughts, and I wouldn't have to say a word. But my camp is used to it. It's only bad if one of the teams gets a broadcast. So, I try not to think too much.

Unfortunately, overthinking is my weakness—

"Jack, shush!" Nico scolds me.

Oops.

We enter the boys' Long Room and walk past rows of bunk beds lining the wall until we reach our shared bunk. I plop down on Nico's bed. Mine is on top; he isn't a fan of heights. Since I'm a Scavenger, I've learned to trust the air over time.

I drop my bag just as the Captain walks in. His sandy-blond hair hangs around his face, and his dark eyes give him a timeless look, as if he's ancient and not just in his late twenties. Nico waves him over, and he strides across the room. I hand over my bag for inspection. He rummages around, finding pieces of metal, cloth, and a few good apples.

The Captain nods to me before leaving the room. "Good work, Barret."

Yes! The Captain rarely hands out approval.

"Thank you, sir."

4

I smile as I take off my boots and coat. I feel so pumped and happy, like I'm finally doing *something* right.

Nico looks at me. "When are Mom and Dad coming home?" he asks.

Our parents are Scouts. They search for better areas to camp and watch out for nearby teams. Their patrol has been gone for three months. We're used to not having them around, or at least I am. Since they're away most of the time, I take care of Nicholas. I love my brother, but an eight-year-old isn't exactly the easiest thing to supervise. I shrug in response to Nico's question, pretending not to see the hurt in his eyes.

Will they ever come back? What if they get captured? Or lost? What if they never come back?

"Jackie, stop!" Nico sighs, and everyone in the room stares at me.

I slump my shoulders as Thomas, one of my best friends, walks over to Nico, places a hand on his shoulder, and replies with absolute certainty, "They will come back."

Thomas acknowledges my look of appreciation with a tight smile. Yet, I can't help feeling guilty that Thomas is a better brother than I am. Of course, Thomas can't broadcast his thoughts. I start to say something to Nico, but the wail of sirens cuts me off.

The Captain storms into the room shouting, "Everyone, get in your hiding positions! This is not a drill!"

The last thing I see before I shove Nico under the bed is the Captain barking orders at someone in the hallway.

5

Chapter II

Friends and Strangers

Being small comes in handy, especially since there's not much space under the bed. I can see everything up to the doorway from where I am. Including the Captain.

And the uncertainty on his face.

I have a sinking suspicion that his emotions aren't his, and that I'm radiating enough panic to make it visible in the Captain's eyes. A place where fear is unheard of. Sometimes I despise my ability. Not only can I broadcast thoughts, but I can project my feelings as well.

I try to make my mind go blank. That's worked before. Not thinking about anything, or focusing on a piece of furniture usually helps, but the only thing in my mind is fear. The Captain walks out of the room. My heart thumps. I'm sure my pulse alone is shaking the floor. A minute goes by, but it feels like an hour. All I know is that by the time the Captain walks back in, I'm sweating from being squished under the bed with Nico.

"False alarm," he assures us. "Only a passing Good team."

Huh.

Teams are similar to our camps, with populations the size of a village or a small town, and made up of mostly adults, teenagers, and sometimes small children. They're nomadic, so it's not shocking that one has blown in. We usually ignore Good teams because they won't harm innocents. But we don't mingle with them, either, unless we're buying supplies or trading with them. Evil teams are a different story. When they pass through towns and cities, they often burn a path of destruction as they go. This is why we hide among buildings and have these drills.

We're on nobody's side but our own, and being friendly with any team shows that we are potential enemies of the other side. We have nothing to do with the eternal war between Goods and Evils, and that's that. I know of other camps with the same ideals as ours, but we barely come into contact with them because of our skill at staying isolated and hidden.

"Dinner's in fifteen minutes," the Captain declares.

Mmm. Everything tastes good when you're hungry. Things are back to normal now, with Nico talking to his little friends and me getting ready for dinner. I take off my jacket and change into more comfortable clothes, throwing the ones I'll need for tomorrow into the shared washer that's situated in front of the connected bathroom, hoping they don't get lost in there.

When fifteen minutes is up, we all file out the door, following Nico to the Dining Hall. It's jam packed, with people from all over our building pouring in through the entrances on all four walls. The Dining Hall is the largest room in the building, right at the core where all paths meet. The wooden tables form rows, and since this is the most open and diverse section of the camp, people track in a lot of strange objects: leaves, dirt, and cloth, for instance.

Long lines snake around the tables and into the kitchen where people are served. The aroma of fresh bread and condensed soup wafts over the lines of people. The cooks use ingredients from outside the camp, like the apples I found, and Scouts trade for grains and meat when on their missions.

7

After getting as much food as I'm allowed, I find a seat next to my best friends, Cali Smith and Thomas Nowak. Cali is twelve. She stays on the other side of camp with the girls. Thomas is my age, and his bunk is next to mine. We've been friends since before Nicholas was born, and we've shared many adventures.

Cali's albino-blond hair glistens in the dim light. She looks like she was born straight out of a happily-ever-after tale, with her dark tan skin, bright hair, electric blue eyes, and graceful features. Thomas, however, has dirty-blond hair, large brown eyes, and a pale skin tone. His ability is Complex, meaning he can work complicated things like knots, machines, and locks. He always carries tools or rope, and I often catch him fiddling with a lock or some little gizmo.

"What?" Thomas asks. I realize that I'm staring at him, still thinking about his ability.

"Nothing!"

"Okay, Jack."

Cali chuckles and changes the subject to the false alarm. She describes how she was ready to send a bunk bed flying out the door. Her ability is MindLift; she can pick up almost anything without using an ounce of her physical strength. Which, in my opinion, is way cooler and way more useful than my ability.

"Jack was making the Captain scared again," Thomas confesses for me.

"Again?" I exclaim. I throw a random pebble at him, and he dodges.

"Don't waste your ammo on me." He laughs. "Use it on intruders."

8

Cali giggles. "You two are ridiculous."

I stand up and give a dramatic bow, with a spoon held firmly between my teeth.

"'Ridiculous' is my middle name," I tell her.

Thomas nudges me and indicates with his eyebrows toward the Captain, who is giving me a stern expression. I sit down and we eat our food quietly.

After dinner, we shuffle back to our designated Long Rooms for curfew. I'm brushing my teeth with my tiny wooden toothbrush, thinking, *How come animals out in the wild don't brush their teeth, but ours will rot if we don't?* when Nico gives me this face that either means I'm broadcasting, or I'm being really obvious and staring at my toothbrush with some strange expression, or maybe both.

When we're done getting ready for bed, I tuck Nico in, making sure his toes are covered by his threadbare blanket. Then I climb up the ladder and into my bed.

"Lights out!" the Captain calls, and soon the lights flicker off, drenching us in an eerie darkness, one that abandons the familiar creaks and conversations of the hallways and rooms.

I hate sleeping. Not because I'm afraid of the dark, but because when I sleep, I always have dreams, and none of them are mine. My ability allows me to travel to other people's dreams, but I don't get to pick whose.

Sleep eventually comes, and *whoosh!* Here I am in the type of beautiful green meadow I've only heard about in stories, much unlike the dull city we live in. In front of me is an older girl with cocoa skin. She's wearing a purple bandana in her frizzy jet-black hair.

Her eyes are closed, but she says, "I must warn him. We must track it down before they do."

Already, I'm getting a creepy vibe because she sounds like she's been expecting me. I usually interrupt people.

"I'm here by accident," I say. "Sorry. Um … Peace."

She opens her eyes, and her fierce gray irises send chills down my spine. "The Beacon! It worked!"

Bacon? What? I try to run but my legs won't move. I look back; the girl is pointing above me. I get the feeling it's some kind of message. Everything goes black for a while.

When I hear a soft scraping noise, I open my eyes. I'm awake. The tiny window above my bed is open, and there's the girl, standing over me.

"Were you stalking me?" I whisper.

She puts her fingers to her lips before grabbing my arm and yanking me out of bed and down the ladder. Let's just say no one has ever accused me of being graceful, so I tumble on top of her. It's too dark to see her, but I can't see my own hand in front of me, either. It's almost as if we disappeared, though I know I'm still in the room, and I sure feel as though I'm sitting on someone's foot.

Then it hits me. We're invisible. That must be her ability. I get up and try to shake her off, but she won't let go of me.

"Come with me," she says. "You're the only one who can find it." Her fingers tighten around my wrist, and she drags me out of the room.

Chapter III

Failed Attempts

Panic makes my throat close, and I realize my ability isn't so bad after all. I think to the girl, *"Hey, who are you? Where are we going?"*

She responds calmly. "I'm Nora Moreau. Don't be scared. You'll understand soon."

That doesn't answer my questions. I enjoy a little adventure now and then, but being kidnapped isn't on the list of things I want to do. I repeat my message, but Nora only pushes forward, still invisible. I'm confident that we're lost, though Nora seems sure of our destination. She holds a stick that, when bent, creates a florescent light that casts shadows.

As we wander the tunnels, I continue to repeat the question. It's obnoxious, but that's the point.

Eventually, we turn a corner and we become visible. She stares me straight in the eye with that fierce expression of hers, and hisses, "We are going to my Good team, the Benevolent Blue Jay. No. More. Questions."

A Good team? No. No way! Nora is invisible again, pulling me, but I stop. *"You're crazy!"* I think at her, trying to pry my wrist from her strong hand.

I can't see it, but she's probably giving me a dirty look. I finally pull away from her grip, and I'm no longer hidden. I hear Nora exhale slowly. I start to back up into the hallway we came from, but an unseen hand clamps over my mouth, pushing me forward.

I try to scream for help, both out loud and in my thoughts. Purposely broadcasting an alert, I concentrate on the hard task of going, *"AHHHHHHHHHHHHHHHHHH."*

It works. Nora is visible and clutching her ears, though barely any sound escaped my mouth. I hope it woke up a few people.

Nora kneels on the floor, her hands still cupped over her ears. "Stop! Please stop!"

I realize I'm still broadcasting. The lights come on, not too bright, just a string of them on the wall. I stop screeching in my thoughts.

Voices echo down the tunnel, shouting, "Jack? Jax! Jackie! Barret?"

It's Thomas, Nico, and the Captain. Nora is crumpled on the floor, still in shock.

"Over here! I got kidnapped, sorta!"

I wait, glancing over my shoulder at the tunnel and back at Nora. I can't believe the Goods are taking us now. Maybe they're desperate for people. Whatever the case, I'm not going to be part of it.

Nico appears around the corner, with Thomas and the Captain close behind. The Captain looks at me, then at Nora, disapproval glittering in his harsh onyx eyes. Thomas and Nico walk over to me, relief shining in their expressions.

"They woke me up from a really good dream and told me you were gone. I thought you left for forever!" Nico whispers to me.

I shake my head; my words won't come, and my thoughts are jumbled. Thomas leans in and says softly,

12

"You shrieked right into my dream. The Captain and a few others were wide awake. Then we saw you were gone. Dude, that was insane! I bet it was loud enough to be heard in Evil headquarters!"

I chuckle, though I hope he's wrong.

The Captain marches over to Nora, grabs her by the arm, and roughly hoists her to her feet. She groans, and the Captain knocks her out with a quick strike to the back of her head. He turns to me and raises his eyebrows.

I mumble about being kidnapped and explain, "She's from a Good team. The Benen ... Benev ... Benevolent Blue Bird? Also, something about breakfast meat. That's all I caught. You might wanna know that her ability is Invisibility. Oh! And her name's Nora. Nora Moreau."

The Captain soaks up the information, mutters about a beacon, then picks up Nora and slings her over his shoulder like a bag of coal.

With Nicholas in the lead, we trudge back through the dim corridors. Our shadows dance along the walls, flickering along to the lights.

Back in the Long Room, almost everyone is sitting up in their bed, or walking around, or chatting. A few are still sleeping. I wonder if they woke up and went back to sleep, or if they're having a strange dream involving the sound of screaming.

As soon as they realize we're back, everything goes silent. Eyes follow us, curious, judging, questioning. I stare right back, and Thomas puts his hand on my shoulder.

The Captain clears his throat. "Everyone back to sleep. Tomorrow is still another day. Even though you have

13

missed a part of your rest," he says with a disapproving glance in my direction, "you still have work to do. And no questions."

The Captain walks out of the room with Nora.

After I tuck Nico in a second time, I climb up into my bunk and wait for the lights to go out. My mind replays the events of the night, over and over. It's kind of strange how the Captain knew what I was talking about when I mentioned bacon, and how he marched in, grabbed Nora, and marched out without a second thought. I respect the Captain, but something seems off. Finally, I let the thought slip from my mind and close my eyes. Though, I'm half-asleep for the rest of the night.

Chapter IV

Scavenger

I open my eyes to the sound of whispers. Little rumors, small voices, big grumbles surrounding me. All I see is the ceiling—pale blue, almost a light shade of gray—above me.

Thomas swings up on the railing of the bunk.

"Rise and shine! Today's a new day for you to get complained at for waking everyone up in the middle of the night," he exclaims.

I turn to him with a dead stare, not completely there. When Nico pops up beside him, my brain goes back to full function: take care of Nicholas, take care of camp. I chuckle to myself, thinking about how much work I do with only two mind-sets—Nico and camp—and no one seems to notice. Of course I love him, but sometimes I wonder if I could do more without the responsibility of taking care of him.

I crawl down the ladder and put on my coat instead of my vest, knowing it will be cold outside. The condensation on the tiny window that Nora came through proves it.

Nora. I wonder what happened to her. I zip up my coat and slide on my usual black leather boots, scruffy like me. Once I have my green scarf around my neck, I grab my bag.

Thomas gets ready to work all over the camp. Lots of people depend on him to help build or take apart machines and fix things. Thomas is strong, so he helps carry boxes to supply rooms, too.

After we finish preparing for work—changing, packing needed tools, and double checking that we have what we need—we wait in lines that organize us into our separate jobs, so the Labyrinth Keepers can guide us to our designated destinations. I wait with the Scavengers, some my age, most a bit younger, and a few adults. Kids under twelve usually tag along with the adults for safety and company. I sometimes help them, but most of the time I work alone.

Some of the adults are passing around food, since we're working all day with no snack break. I take some beef jerky, hoping it will be enough to sustain me until dinner. We rarely eat breakfast or lunch in the camp.

Once everyone is ready, Nico tells us to follow him, and we're off into the tunnels. I climb out of the hatch with the others, and we all scatter in different directions.

I leap off our building and tuck into a roll, landing and sliding down a tilted roof. The wind slaps my face, chilly, yet nice. Freedom. Scavenging is one of the only jobs that allows us to roam outside all day, outside of camp, away from the cramped rooms and claustrophobic hallways. Outside, I'm in control.

I sprint easily down the elevated catwalks and roofs, getting closer to the ground with every jump. There isn't much left of the damaged city, but the sheer size of it, along with passing teams and freak winds bringing in new items and supplies, provides just enough for camp. Our city is small compared to other places, yet it's huge to us.

Thinking of passing teams, I wonder if Nora's is out here. I decide to lie low in a more secluded part of the city, away from the streets and roofs. I jump into an alley, finally on solid ground. A little exploration can't hurt.

The alley is dull, like the rest of the city, with piles of junk and scrap metal lining every corner. Tiny noises squeak and creak in harmony with the quiet drone of our forgotten world. We're just another creature trying to survive in the busy bustle of the universe.

I enjoy scavenging because I get to wander alone with my thoughts, without the anxiety of broadcasting. There's a lot less pressure when others aren't constantly around me. And strangely enough, I don't broadcast as often when I'm alone.

I load small bits of metal and pipe into my bag as I pass from street to street. A Scavenger's bag is spacious, sturdy, and easy to hold. It goes over my shoulders and fastens at the chest and waist, sort of like a backpack mixed with a harness. Even though I'm small and scrappy, I've gotten quite strong from scrambling around the buildings and carrying a heavy bag full of supplies. I make sure to pick up the bigger stuff later on.

I scurry around the alleys, trying my best to stay away from the cracked roads, taking turns I usually avoid since they're out of the way. The streets are in the open, and I could be spotted by someone or something, even when there aren't any known teams around. I keep my head and shoulders low, and I slink along, picking up whatever seems useful or valuable. As I go, I snack on my bits of jerky until it's all gone. I grab bigger sheets of metal and pipes, unloading the smaller items to make enough room, then packing everything back up again.

Turning what I think is a familiar corner, I'm suddenly in a small jungle of pipes and tubes. I've never

17

been here before. It's a maze, with pieces of pipe and metal sticking out all over the place, blocking my way.

I throw my bag into a space and squeeze through behind it, using my feet to propel me through the small entry. Past several other gaps, I end up in front of a giant rusty pipe.

Something in my gut tugs me toward the dark entrance, encouraging me to climb in. Being the smart guy I am, I get on my knees and crawl inside, head-first, without checking for any hazards, dragging my bag along behind me. It's dark, so I fish a light bulb the size of my thumb out of my coat pocket. I flick it on and hold it by its cord with my mouth.

I inch through the pipe until it slopes upwards dramatically. I'm thinking, *Well, this must be the end*, when I notice rungs.

It can't hurt to explore a bit more, so I pull my bag around my shoulders, grasp the highest rung I can reach, and lift myself up. It's hard to climb due to the heavy load, the cramped space, and my aching back, but I push myself.

When I reach the top, my little light flickers. I can feel that the pipe has led me into a spacious room by the empty air around me. At the far end of the room, something glitters. I squint and rub my eyes to make sure I'm not hallucinating. A soft aquamarine light illuminates the floor and the walls nearest the source. There's a dip in the floor, like a basin, where the strange light is coming from.

Sweat trickles down my forehead as I walk a step, then stop. I admit to myself that I'm a little scared. I'm not usually afraid of the dark, but unknown darkness? I don't know. Especially with what happened last night.

18

My heart beats to the rhythm of the water I hear dripping nearby. Something is running, but not *running-running*, more a *drip-drip-drip-dripping*. A strong mix of yearning and exhilaration, a longing for adventure, rises up in me. So, instead of calling it quits, I decide to be brave. Curiosity wins.

I slowly tiptoe over to the edge of the pit. The eerie color draws my attention; I can't take my eyes off it. My mind is completely silent, though there's a faint buzz in the air. I carefully lower myself into the pit, though it's deeper than I thought. I end up dropping a couple of feet, landing on my side. A cool sensation spreads around my elbow. There's a pool of water at the bottom of the pit.

At the far end is a thick glass hatch with a tiny checkered pattern and a handle. Water slips through a pinhole at the top and runs down the face of the hatch onto the floor, into the pool. The inside of the hatch ripples and glitters, casting green-blue waves of light that reflect off the glass. The droplets echo on the floor. My mouth hangs open in awe, and I almost drop the light bulb, but manage to catch it between my teeth.

I mean, I've seen water before, but the way this water glows is something magical. *There must be a precious treasure inside!*

Now, I'm not the brightest person, so like an idiot, I forget there's water inside. I grab the handle and tug the hatch off. Ice-cold water slams into me—a lot more than I expected.

I fall back on my behind, and the freezing water sends a chilling shock through my body and pushes at my legs. The torrent hits me in the face, along with a hard object. It's an aqua-colored stone, but it's shining, and now I know what drew me here.

I snatch up the stone as the current pushes me under the water. Everything becomes a blue blur now that my light has gone off.

Panicking, I flail my arms around until I get my feet under me. The water reaches my shoulders, but at least I can breathe. Clutching the weird rock, I try to float to the rim of the basin, but I can't reach the top yet. The ice-cold water floods out of the open hatch, faster and faster, rising and rising.

I try to take a step toward the rim of the pit, but the hatch knocks against the back of my legs. My knees buckle, and I'm submerged again.

Chapter V

Treasure

My heart skips a beat. I'm in shock. I can't get up. Not with the current forcing me under the darkness.

The stone fits perfectly in my palm, its faint outline is visible through my fingers. It's as though I'm holding another hand, sturdy and strong. A sense of reassurance warms me. Not as helpless now, I'm infused with hope and the instinct to survive.

I fight the raging torrent, kicking and punching the water, trying to move myself along. The water is rising and swirling around, but I don't seem to get very far. And my breath is running out. I twist and thrash around blindly, trying to escape and swim up and out of the pit.

Then I realize why I'm stuck. A jagged piece of metal on the hatch is snagged on my pants, near my knee. I try to shake it free, but it won't budge. Even the mighty water can't loosen it.

My chest burns. My arms and legs ache. My head becomes a balloon under pressure, light, fragile, ready to pop any minute. I want to give up.

I close my eyes. The current doesn't feel as crazy, more like a gentle tug. Like hands lifting me away. Like the balloon is floating through the sky. Like I'm melting but not burning, just liquefying.

I see Nico, Thomas, Cali, and my parents. *Have you come to say goodbye?*

I open my eyes and the water is still grabbing me. Aquamarine bubbles rush past my face. I'm not drifting. I'm being drowned forcefully by this stupid water and my own curiosity and ambition. The lack of peacefulness makes me angry. The water won't let me float quietly. No. Instead, it interrupts my peace of mind and slaps me in the face.

Then, I see the stone.

A surge of adrenaline fills me with energy and momentarily stalls my pain, encouraging me to kick with all my might. My pants rip. Something digs into my skin and lets go. I pull free from the thing that tried to drown me. The water is above my head; I swim to the surface.

I gasp in a giant breath. And another. I breathe. Just breathe. I float over to the rim of the pit, climb out, and roll over onto my back in a wet pile, catching my breath. My lungs feel like icicles. Cold and sharp.

But I remember that I have work to do, and my job isn't to explore and almost die in weird pipe rooms. My job is to scavenge. I need to help my camp. I need to supply them. Without me and the other Scavengers, our camp would be in shambles, starving.

I roll back over and stand up. My light is gone, but the stone provides enough luminosity to see. I stagger over to the pipe in the floor and carefully lower my foot to the first rung, then to the next.

When I reach the bottom, I crawl out slowly into the light. I plunk my bag down and sit against the pipe, soaked and chilled to the bone. When I try to get up, I wince and stumble to the ground, my leg burning. I peer down at my shredded pants. A gash runs from the side of my knee down to my ankle. It doesn't look too bad, but it hurts like crazy.

I'm sore, battered, bruised, and bleeding, but I feel lucky to be alive. A lot of people with similar jobs to mine don't come back—not in one piece, anyway. Many Evil teams take hostages, and though I've never seen anything strange, I've heard rumors of mutated creatures and Evil-controlled robots patrolling broken cities like mine. If you're smart, trouble can be easily avoided. Except I'm not very smart. But the experience wasn't *so* bad; I got a glowing stone as my consolation prize.

I take off my soaked coat and shiver. I wring it out and put it back on—it's better than nothing. There's some cloth in my bag; I take it out and wrap it around my wound. It stings, but I don't want it to get infected.

The bag of materials seems to have gotten heavier since my ordeal, but I lug it back to camp, still holding the stone, leaving a trail of water behind me. It appears to be a precious treasure. It glows, so it must be something of value, and the weight of it in my palm is satisfying. It's glossy with little patterns cutting grooves in the surface. As I trudge along, I gaze up at the once proud skyscrapers, now dilapidated and miserable-looking. They reflect the condition of our society now.

Along the way, I take a huge canteen from my bag and fill it with water at a reservoir that I stop at regularly. We only get water a few times a day at camp, but there are no rules against keeping our own water. I'll ask Cali to take it to the kitchen to be purified or whatever, since she helps out in there sometimes. As long as it's drinkable.

I'm not too far from camp now. The sun will set soon. Temperatures at night in the city are always chillier than during the day, and weird things lurk the roads in the dark.

I make my way up through a series of platforms, ladders, and stairs, both on the sides of buildings and inside. The ladders are ice-cold, so I try to find stairs inside more often. I clench my teeth because of the pain in my leg, but I don't stop moving. Finally, I'm on the roof of our building. Too exhausted to climb down the ladder with my bag, I take it off and drop it down the opening. It lands with a *clank.*

Predictably, Nico's inside, scampering up to the bag. I step on the first rung and lower myself down as carefully as possible.

"Jackie! You look absolutely *terrible*," Nicholas gasps.

"Thanks."

"What in the world did you crawl out of?"

"A giant pipe," I answer.

He wrinkles his nose and says, "No, seriously."

Exhaling, I sink to the floor. I hold out my hand and open my fist, revealing the stone. Nico's jaw drops. His eyes reflect the light of the stone.

"This is what I found in the pipe," I explain, wrapping my fingers around it. "Well, actually, the pipe led to a room with a hatch. Full of water. I almost drowned."

"What?" he shrieks.

Immediate regret sinks into my stomach for adding my near-death experience. It's a known fact that he worries about me, and I hate giving him an extra burden to carry. He deserves better.

"Don't fret. It wasn't that bad. I just got tangled is all."

Of course, the words seem empty to him now that he's noticed my bleeding leg. With a grunt, he picks up my bag and helps me up. I try not to lean on him too much as we walk through the tunnels, but his support is both helpful and reassuring—I made it back to see my brother again.

After what feels like forever, we make it to the Long Room. By that time, I'm almost dead with exhaustion. My muscles ache and tremble, not to mention the throbbing in my leg. My stomach churns, since the only thing I've eaten is my own fear and some jerky. I stagger over to a chair and collapse, shivering.

The room is mostly empty, with a few people coming in or lounging around. Nico asks some of the older boys to help find the Captain, and I doze off on the chair, which is now soaked.

I wake up to someone shaking my arm. The Captain studies me with a stern yet concerned expression. For a second, I forget what happened and why he's all up in my business. Then I remember.

"I just can't seem to leave you alone, Barret. One moment you get kidnapped in your sleep, the next you're drowning and getting cuts from who knows where," the Captain says in a light tone, though I know he's serious.

My gut twists with apprehension, and a bad taste settles in the back of my mouth. For some reason, I think I shouldn't show him the stone, so I slip it into my pocket, no big deal.

"The doctor is out helping set a broken arm right now, so you may have to wait a bit," the Captain tells me. "I'll be back as soon as I hear from him."

He walks out, shouting at someone in the hall.

Nico pulls a chair up in front of me. "I'm on break now."

I smile, despite the pain in my leg. We rarely get free time together.

"Wanna play Five Seconds to Answer while we wait for the Captain to come back?" he asks.

I nod.

Five Seconds to Answer is a game we made up to pass time. The rules are simple. We each take turns asking random questions, and the person being questioned has to answer in, well, five seconds or less.

"I'll go first," Nico says, then pauses, thinking of a question. "All right, what's the last animal you've seen while outside?"

"A bird," I answer automatically, thinking of a giant brown bird soaring over the city a month ago.

"Okay, ask me one!"

"Hmm." I try to think of something that might stump him. Nicholas has such a good memory, that I can't ask something he might not remember. Still, this is a good way to train his mind, even if that means I lose all the time.

"How many windows are on the third floor?" I ask.

"Seven on the north side, five on the south," he says, not skipping a beat.

I chuckle. "You're good."

26

We go on playing the game, with him winning every round, until the Captain walks back in.

"The doctor just got back in his office. We can head down there now," he says.

Nico jumps up and waits at the doorway for us.

The Captain asks me if I'm able to walk, and I tell him that I'm fine, everything's fine, but then he tries to wrap my leg in a fresh cloth, and I grumble and complain loudly that it's not fine.

Nico leads the Captain and I down a few flights of stairs. I'm leaning on the Captain and hopping on one foot down the steps. We pass the occasional bathroom and storage room, as well as many offices where the monitors and older workers who help out sleep. I think about the Captain taking Nora away last night, never to be seen or heard from again. When I ask if they let her go, the Captain sighs and nods, telling me he doesn't want any trouble with the Goods.

We end up in the medicine room, and the doctor wraps up my leg and gives me all sorts of disgusting stuff to swallow, but it helps fight the pain. Nico leaves the room to get cleaned up for dinner, and the doctor explains that I need to keep the wound wrapped or else the ointment will come off and it will get infected blah, blah, blah. The doctor departs as well, leaving me alone with the Captain.

It's been long enough for the medication to kick in, and I'm feeling pretty good about myself until the Captain says, "I heard you found a glowing rock."

A shock arcs through my body. He might as well have slapped me. Did Nico tell him?

27

The Captain's face betrays no emotion or sign of how he found out.

"So, let's see it, Barret."

Chapter VI

Into the Dark

"S—see what?" I stammer.

No way. *No way!* How does he know? My hands clench in my pockets.

"The little rock you found," he replies calmly, like he knew I would react nervously.

I give an innocent smile, but I can tell he knows. "Did you say a … glowing rock? Where'd you hear about that?" I ask feebly, trying to buy myself time to think.

He frowns. "That's none of your concern, Barret."

I only stare at him, thinking it should be my concern; I'm the one who found the thing in the first place. But I don't like the way he calls it a rock, as if he doesn't believe it and is just pretending that it's not a cool valuable. Like the weird glowing stone isn't more than a weird glowing stone.

I stand. Dishonesty has never been one of my strengths, but I don't want to be rude.

"I'm sorry, sir," I say, chuckling nervously. "Now that you mention it, I do recall seeing something shiny, though not a glowing stone, but my main priority was to, y'know, not die. Uh, so if you'll please excuse me …"

I move to walk around him, but he puts a firm hand on my shoulder.

"Barret, this will be a lot easier if you just give me the rock. You obviously don't know what it is. Well, I'll tell you now, this device is not your ordinary pebble. Now ..."

He takes his hand off my shoulder and opens his palm for me to put the stone in. My mouth twitches, as though it can't decide whether to keep smiling or not. He obviously saw through my lie, and honestly, giving him the stone is probably a lot safer. But something doesn't feel right. The Captain knew about beacons, he took Nora, and now he's making a big deal over a rock. I look up at the Captain, seeing him in a whole new light. And then I make my choice.

It's like I'm possessed. Instead of obeying, I duck under his outstretched arm and squeeze past him into the dark hallway. My body goes on autopilot, the stone seems to glow brighter in my pocket, which completely disproves my lie. Footsteps pound behind me, and I feel his fingertips on the collar of my coat. *Well, I stopped Nora. I can totally stop the Captain.*

Right as he grabs my collar, I aim my broadcast at him and screech, *"EEEEEEEEEEEK."* Startled, he lets go.

I run as fast as I can, barely feeling anything in my leg. I manage to sprint up the stairs like some crazed animal, using my hands to boost me. I turn the corner, not looking back.

Only the light of the stone filtering out of my pocket allows me to see. Around the next corner, dim lanterns shine at the end of the hall. I rush toward them, then pause at a fork. Now which way? Both tunnels are identical, but one could lead to the kitchen and the other outside.

No time to think about it. I take a deep breath and charge into the left tunnel. I scramble down the hallway and suddenly crash into something at the corner. Landing on my behind, I look up, more dazed than hurt.

"Cali!"

She stares at me in surprise and disbelief.

"Jack? Where were you? You missed dinner!" she says, helping me up to my feet.

I explain what happened while I was scavenging: the water, the stone, and everything after that. As I tell her, her eyes widen, bigger and bigger.

"So ... you mean to tell me that the boys' captain is evil?"

I shake my head. "No, no. But he is up to something. Maybe the entire camp is up to something. He called the stone a device, like some sort of tech."

"Oh."

"Can I trust you to not help him take the stone?" I ask, though it's more of a plea.

"Of course!"

She forces open a nearby door and pulls me inside the room. Cali puts her fingers to her lips and whispers, "*Shh* ... Everyone's coming back from dinner, but I headed back early since you were missing and Thomas was held back from dinner to work on something. The girls' Long Room is near the Dining Hall, so I memorized the way back."

The room is dark, but I realize where we are immediately.

"I can't be in here!" I hiss.

Cali chuckles. "It's okay. We're the only ones here. You need a place to hide until we can figure out what to do."

I consider two options. The first is to go to the Adults' Quarters and maybe find some help there. It's in the building next to ours, but I'm sure if we find Nico, we'll be able to get there. Once you reach the age of seventeen, you no longer need to stay in the Youth Quarters. You can choose to leave, or live with the other adults, or family, or friends, or maybe get a family, stuff like that. We could go to that place. The second option is to leave the camp. I'm not too fond of the second one.

Cali grabs my arm and guides me to what I'm assuming is her bunk.

"I'm sure you can fit under there, right?" she asks.

I push myself under the bed and try not to whimper as my bandaged leg brushes past the wooden edge. Creaking sounds tell me Cali is moving around on her bunk, right above my head.

My stomach rumbles. I sigh hungrily.

Suddenly. a stampede outside crashes into the room, accompanied by the excited chatter of girls. I scrunch myself farther under the bunk, into the darkness. That's harder since the lights came on.

A painfully long thirty minutes of listening to girls' gossip passes before I hear a deeper female voice go, "Lights out!" The dark and quiet follow soon after.

Cali must have forgotten my existence, as most people do.

I realize I should stop thinking—I'm not good at keeping my thoughts to myself. I close my eyes and make my mind go blank.

A few seconds, or maybe a few hours later, I jolt awake at something beeping softly. It shuts off and the bunk above me lifts. I almost have a heart attack thinking that somebody with superhuman strength found me. But it's just Cali standing next to the levitating bed.

I slide out and Cali slowly places the bunk down. It lands with a soft *thud*. We tiptoe out of the room, leaving the snores and calmness behind.

She stops to face me, smiles, and whispers, "Sorry you had to wait so long. Some of the girls take a couple of hours to fall asleep, so I set an alarm under my pillow so I wouldn't forget to get you."

"It's okay. We need to find Nico. Then we can go to the Adults' Quarters and look for help."

"And if no one can help us?" she murmurs.

"Let's hope someone can," I reply, not wanting to think about option two.

We pad down the corridor. I pull the stone out of my pocket for light. Cali gasps quietly, her face illuminated by the soft aqua glow. I smile. We follow the tunnel, reassured by the warm presence of the stone as we descend into darkness.

Chapter VII

Vision

We inch blindly through the night, like worms in their underground tunnels. The thought sends chills up my spine.

Cali whispers beside me, "Where are we, Jack?"

Like I would know. I feel her panic and urgency. We need to move, fast, before we're found.

The stone is warm in my palm, and it's getting warmer and warmer. I open my hand to find the stone is brighter than the freshest light bulb.

Cali backs away from me in fear, and I know I'm in trouble. Anything that scares a girl like Cali, definitely terrifies a person like me.

I can't drop the stone, even though it feels as though I'm holding the outside of a lantern that's been burning for hours. I try to shake the stone out of my hand, but it sticks to my palm and fingers. I yelp and fall to my knees just as everything goes a shade of blue and green.

The weightlessness of drifting in the water back in the pipe room returns. But this time, I'm in control. I'm not being pushed around, and there's nothing pinning me down. I feel free.

I'm able to see clearly in the hallway; everything has this eerie glow. I see Cali, but she's made up of a strong bluish light, most of it where her head is. I see myself, crumpled on the floor, and my body is infused with the same kind of light as Cali, most of it concentrated at my head as well. But combined with the stone in my hand, the light is stronger, pulsing brightly. A series of images floods my mind, and I understand that the lights resemble our abilities. The stone isn't a rock, but a device. But what's it for?

I drift over to my body. I lean down and poke it experimentally, and then I'm back. The lights are gone.

I roll over on my side, groaning. I drop the stone. My hand is red and steaming. It doesn't hurt now because it's numb, but sooner or later I'll feel it. That'll be fun.

Cali kneels down next to me, mumbling, "Oh my gosh. Oh my gosh. Jack, oh my gosh."

Sitting up, I blink away the stars.

"Okay, that thing is dangerous, Jack," Cali says, pointing to the stone.

My hand starts to feel like someone is deep-frying it in oil.

"You need to put it back where you found it," Cali adds.

Frowning, I get up slowly and shake my head.

"No," I say. "It's like … I don't know, some super crazy tech that relates to our abilities. We can't let it fall into the wrong hands."

Okay, so maybe I'm not the best at explaining things, but I just got out of this freaky vision, and I'm at a loss for words. I snatch up the stone, and suddenly my hand goes from being fried to being slightly charred. The pain subsides, and I clench the stone tighter. Simply holding it makes me feel safe. Knowing some of the things it can do, I can't help feeling that if anyone else had it, especially the Evils, the world would get a lot more dangerous.

Cali balls her fist, staring me directly in the eye.

"And who are the right hands? You think that's *us*?" she growls.

"Cali, please. Maybe we're not meant to have it, and maybe we are. But we do have it. I can't explain it, but this is important. This changes everything."

She sighs and nods. "Fine."

"C'mon," I say, exhaling.

I start walking and Cali follows me. We travel through the tunnels in silence until we come across an open door that sheds light out into the hallway. I slip the stone into my pocket and creep along the wall to the door.

Inside the room, Nora is sitting on a bench. Her hands are tied in front of her with a rope that's connected to the wall. There's nothing else in the room, just the bench, the light on the ceiling, and Nora's shadow stretching down the thin gray wall. I'm sure I've passed by it a few times with Nico. It appears to be an empty storage closet. I look back at Cali. *Wait here,* I tell her with a simple hand gesture. She nods.

Not seeing anyone else in the room, I sneak inside.

"Nora! *Psst,* Nora!" I hiss.

She regards me with a pleased expression, like she was waiting for me.

"What are you doing here?" I whisper, a little shocked. The Captain *lied* to me about Nora's whereabouts.

Motioning to her bindings, she replies, "A man took me here—one with blond hair and black eyes. He told me, 'I believe I know why you're here. Just know, whatever you're looking for, you won't find it at this camp. You must stay here until the leaders have decided what to do with you, though know you are most certainly not welcome here.' Jack, I promise I'm on your side."

"How do you know my name?"

"Everyone was shouting it in the tunnel," Nora explains.

I narrow my eyes and cross my arms, trying to give her the silent message that I don't trust her whatsoever. She's made a pretty bad impression so far: all in one night, she tried to kidnap me and take me to her camp, and now—

"You're not on my side," I snap. "You're on the Good side. The man was right, too. You can't have the stone."

Nora's gaze lights up and shoots toward my pocket. I turn so she can't see the glow, but it's too late.

"So, you retrieved it. Good, good. But Jack, you must listen to me. *They* are coming. Your camp can't protect you any longer. They're coming for you and it, which is exactly why you'll need my help."

"Well ... You're being very vague. Who's 'they'?"

She doesn't respond, but instead stares at me with what I think is pity. My heart races. Someone's after me? Why? No one knows me. Does she mean the Captain? Probably not. I'm in the background. I'm not ... special. Just lucky. Or cursed, depending on how you look at it.

But a little thought in the back of my head floats forward.

Don't you want to be? Don't you wish you were special? Important?

I'm not answering that.

"What's so special about me?" I say.

"You may not realize this, but the fate of the world rests in your hands. There's only one person with an ability like yours—you. There's only one stone, and it's capable of so much more than you think."

Nora's words are a lot to process. But she doesn't allow me any time to think them over.

She holds out her wrists for me.

"The man will be back. I'll explain later, but help me now so I can help you," she says urgently.

I consider the pros and cons of helping Nora. She's a Good; she wouldn't lie to me, right? Not like I have any experience with teams. But I recall how the Captain didn't hesitate to try and deceive me about Nora, then I think about Nora's words about the possible future. I come to the hasty conclusion that because Nora knows more about this than I do, maybe she can help me figure out what's going on. I scan the room for something sharp. No way can I untie those knots. That's Thomas's job.

I hold up my hands and say, "I don't have a knife with me."

Nora smiles. "That's okay. Take out the stone."

"Why?"

"Just do it, Jack. We don't have all night."

Confused, I take the stone out of my pocket. I decide to believe Nora, knowing she probably has a better plan than simply running away.

Can the stone melt rope? That would be messy. Suddenly, the stone flashes and comes apart. I curse, thinking that it's broken, but the pieces form links and the links form a handle and jutting out of that handle is a blade. Now, instead of a glowing aqua stone, I'm holding a small glowing aqua knife.

"Well, don't just stand there," Nora sighs.

I close my mouth, swallow my awe, and cut the bindings. The knife passes through the rope like butter.

Nora stands, and I immediately regret my decision to help. Like most people, she's taller than me, and unlike most people, she gives me a mischievous smirk that makes me wonder if she's part of a Good team or an Evil one. She rubs the back of her head and stretches.

The knife folds back into the stone. I drop it back into my pocket and follow Nora out the door.

"Thought you'd never come out," Cali grumbles. She looks up. "Who's that?"

Nora introduces herself and marches off into the tunnel.

"Do you even know where you're going?" Cali calls after her.

Cali's right, we don't know where we are, and we've lived here for years. Nora's only been here for a day.

I nod. "We have to find my brother. He knows the camp like the back of his hand. That *was* our initial plan."

"Then I suppose we'll have to find him." Nora turns toward a new tunnel, leaving us no choice but to follow.

Chapter VIII

Jitters

Our building is big, and it feels like we've been wandering forever. Maybe we're going in circles. It's too dark in the halls to see any of my brother's notes, and I wonder if they're even there. My internal clock tells me that it's a few hours after midnight, now very early morning. I hope we can get out of here before dawn, that is, unless we're found by the Captain or someone in charge before everyone wakes up. All I hope is that we're far away from him now.

We follow Nora around the thousandth corner when she stops, causing me to crash into her and Cali to crash into me.

"What gives?" Cali hisses with annoyance.

I blink. The hallway is still quite dim, but the shadows are rising as if a light were near us. That's not good. But at least we can somewhat see.

Nora turns around to face us, her eyes gleaming in the dark.

"There's someone coming," she hisses.

Cali sighs with frustration. Knowing her, she probably sees this as a minor disturbance.

Nora holds out her hand and whispers, "Grab hands, and don't let go."

I hesitantly lock hands with the girls, placing my right in Nora's and my left in Cali's. Cali gasps as we all disappear.

The tension and discomfort of holding hands with two girls is probably what's making my palms sweaty. Gross, right? Well, it's worse because the air is warm from vents that control the temperature, and we're moving, and then I feel like I'm choking because my brain decided to make me aware of my breathing.

Or maybe it's the weird chills I'm getting.

Or maybe my hands are disgusting and sweaty, and I'm paranoid about being human.

A small, scared voice calls out from the end of the tunnel. We all jump.

"Jackie?"

I snatch my hands away from Nora and Cali and rush toward the light at the end of the tunnel. Someone tries to reach for me, but I sprint down the corridor, no longer invisible, ignoring the pain spiking down my leg.

Nicholas has a small light bulb clutched in his hand. I bear hug him.

Even though he's almost as big as me, he looks small and lost in the hallway. Nico appearing to need help to navigate the endless number of halls is unnerving, since that's his job.

I remember that the Captain knew about the stone, and I pull away from Nico to glare at him.

"H—how could you tell him?" My voice wavers with anger.

"Tell who—"

"The Captain," I say, cutting him off through gritted teeth. "About the glowing stone."

Nico tilts his head, his eyes wide. I hear the light footsteps of Nora and Cali behind me, but I keep my gaze trained on my brother.

"But I didn't say *anything* to anyone about it, Jax!"

I frown. Then how did the Captain know? Did he see it? Was he expecting it? I try to put the pieces together. The Captain calling it a device. Nora's conversation with the man who tied her up. It still doesn't make any sense. I exhale. My mind hurts from tripping over all these confusing gaps. Cali and Nora appear beside me.

Cali steps forward and says, "Nico, we need you. Can you take us to the Adults' Quarters?"

Nico nods, but Nora interjects. "We can't tell anyone what's happening. Especially about the tech Jack found. It will only cause a panic."

I raise my eyebrows. Since when was she the boss of us?

"Come along," Nora instructs. "We need to move."

"Where are we going?" Nico asks.

"Outside. To my team. Can you show us the exit?"

I stop. Cali and Nico follow my example. Why does she keep insisting we go to the Goods? She knows we're not part of the teams. She won't change our minds. At least, she won't change mine.

Nico says to her simply, "We can't join a Good team."

I wait for Nora to react, but she never gets the chance. A few loud crashes rip through the night. Warning

lights flash and sirens sound and ubiquitous chaos floods
the camp.

Chapter IX

Escape

Nora pushes us through corridors and rooms, telling Nico to go faster. Screams pierce the thin, shaking walls. It feels like an earthquake, only those don't ever happen. My canteen of water, hanging on my belt, bounces with each step I take. One voice echoes above the others.

"Bring it to me!" the voice commands.

We explode down a tunnel, no longer trying to be silent. People stand in the hallways now, some panicked, some confused. There isn't a thing they can do to stop the pandemonium.

Nico yells, "We need to get out of here!"

Yeah, no duh.

"Follow me!" Nico dashes off.

We run past a giant doorway—the boys' Long Room. I look in and see Thomas. We lock eyes and I scramble away, afraid that one of the other kids will see me.

With Nicholas in the lead, we dash into hallways and climb stairs and ramps, gradually going up levels. Only after a few minutes do I realize that Thomas is right behind us.

Finally, we enter a room with a ladder leading up to a trapdoor—one the Scavengers depart from.

I push Cali up first, yelling, "Go! Go! Go!"

Nico goes next, then Thomas, and Nora ahead of me.

I'm right at the top when a hand grips my foot. I try to yank my leg away, but they won't let go. I shake my leg, but the fingers dig in harder. Which hurts. A lot.

Given no other choice, I bust through the hatch into the bleached moonlight, pulling the person up with me.

Cali shouts, "Who the pobblebonk is that?"

Free of the hand, I get up and turn to see who clung to my boot. A skinny kid, a few years older than me, wearing all black, emerges behind me. His hair is a dusty-brown mess with faint purple and red streaks in it. His dark indigo eyes glitter with malice, and his mouth is covered by a worn black scarf. He's pale, with a pink scar that runs diagonally across the bridge of his nose.

I step back, startled.

Nora growls, "Travis. What are you doing here?"

"What does it look like? Besides, I could ask you the same question."

Confused, I look back and forth between them. Nora knows this guy? She doesn't seem to like him. Travis, as she called him, pulls a strange rectangular object out of his pocket and speaks a few words into it.

Nora comes at him like an eagle, swooping down ferociously, swiping the device out of his hands. He doesn't react. She drops it and stomps on it for good measure, shattering the plastic into a million pieces beneath her boot.

"I just took them off your tail so you don't get caught," Travis explains calmly from under his scarf, his voice betraying no emotion.

"Yeah, right," Nora retorts. "I bet you sold our position."

I suddenly realize what's happening. The intruders are coming. We need to block the exit. I grab a nearby crate and throw it at the hatch with all my might. Thomas and Cali spring into action, tackling Travis. Nico helps me block the trapdoor with boxes and planks we find close by.

Out of the corner of my eye, I see Thomas fly away from Travis and land dangerously near the edge. Nora pins down Travis, her forearm on his throat.

I grab Thomas. Someone inside is trying to force the hatch open, so Thomas, Nico, and I sit on the boxes, using our combined weight to keep it closed. Cali uses her ability to move a huge metal crate over. We hop off the trapdoor just as she crushes the wooden boxes with it.

Nora yanks Travis up, her fingers closed around his scarf. "We have to move," she says. "The Evils will be up here soon."

Nico gasps at the word "Evils," and Travis mutters unkind things to Nora. She drags him along, but he doesn't fight.

We follow Nora across the flat roof to the edge, gazing up at the dark sky that now glitters with stars.

"It's so beautiful," Cali exhales.

Nico, Thomas, and Cali haven't seen much of the outside world, apart from through the few windows in the building, or on uncommon occasions when the camp ventured outside. I'm amazed as well, since I've never seen the sky at this time of day.

"Nora," Travis starts. "Will you let go of—"

"Why should I trust you?" Nora snarls. "Why shouldn't I just throw you off this building? I'm sure that's what you would do to me, you *traitor*!"

Travis winces, and I can see in his dark eyes that Nora's words cut deep. Cali steps forward, and Nora's glare softens a bit.

"Of course, it wouldn't be very *Good* of me to toss you off the roof," she murmurs.

Thomas holds out a piece of rope, and Nora nods. She holds Travis by his coat collar, and Thomas wraps the rope around Travis's arms, pinning them to his sides. He finishes off the improvised straitjacket with what I assume is his strongest knot. Nora takes the little bit of rope hanging from the knot and uses it as a leash to tug Travis along. It's pitiful.

"You know this isn't necessary," Travis mutters.

But no one pays him any attention.

Nora leaps from building to building. I'll give her credit—she does it while lugging Travis along in his unfortunate rope situation. On the larger jumps, Nora carries him. Why are we even taking him? It doesn't make sense to me, but Nora seems to have some connection to him, and as long as she's dealing with him, it doesn't really bother me. I'm nervous being out in the city before sunrise. It's dark except for the stars and moon, which shines down on us proudly.

Everyone struggles to follow Nora's speed. Thomas, Cali, and Nico are hesitant to leap off buildings, especially Nico, who's terrified of falling.

I help, of course, giving Thomas and Cali parkour tutorials. I show them that some of the buildings are close enough together that a gigantic step is enough to get across. Other buildings are farther apart, but it seems to comfort them somewhat. In the end, Thomas carries Nico.

There's no point asking Nora where we're going. After our other arguments, it's obvious. Her team. I don't mind, though, because I figure the Goods will want to help us with the Evil invasion, anyway.

After what could be an hour of jogging on the roofs through the sharp winds, we make it to ground level. The air is frigid, colder than in the daytime, and I rub my palms together for warmth. Thomas shivers and mutters to himself about the cold. He, Cali, and Nico are all wearing light clothing—just sweatshirts and pants with boots similar to mine.

Cali hums a tune as we journey, which is something she does when she's anxious or in thought. To my surprise, Travis is the first to join in. Then Nico starts, and after a while I pick up the tune. Thomas follows along, and finally, Nora hums a little harmony.

I decide that maybe our world isn't so messed up after all, if people like us with tons of differences can be brought together with one song.

After following Nora a while longer, I realize that I'm wrong.

Chapter X

Sacrifices

We round a corner and Nora gasps. All of us step forward, staring in horror, our song forgotten.

Burned wood, rubble, and bodies lie before us. I step in front of Nico, trying to shield him from the worst of the tragedy. The smell of smoke makes my nose burn. Nora walks into the destruction and falls on her knees. Cali covers her mouth in shock. Travis's rope hangs limp, but he just stands there and stares at the ruins. Thomas shakes his head sadly. Who would have done such a thing?

I imagine this place used to be an empty center, nestled neatly in between the tallest buildings. Perfect for a Good team to make shelter. Now it's wrecked. Gone.

Travis is expressionless, watching our reactions with no regret, fear, happiness, or anger. I want to strangle him. Only Evils could have done this.

Nora whispers, "The Blue Jay has fallen."

She fishes a blue pendant out of her pocket and sets it in the hand of a lady as a memorial.

"Maybe some of them escaped?" I suggest weakly.

Nora gets up and walks back to us, her eyes stormy and wet. She grabs Travis by his scarf and growls, "Why? You did this, didn't you? What is wrong with you?"

Nico flinches behind me, and I turn to put my hand on his shoulder. Cali and Thomas exchange glances.

"I wasn't here for this," Travis explains. "You think I wanted this to happen? It's not like I could stop it. Besides, we split into two groups, so one Evil team made a sweep of the entire city while I was on the patrol back at their building."

"Is this what's going to happen to our camp?" Cali asks.

Travis shrugs.

Nora releases her grip on him and angrily pushes him back.

"So, what now?" Thomas asks.

"We have a change of plans," Nora replies with a shaky voice. "I think we should—" She stops abruptly and whips around, holding out her hand for silence. I pause, straining my ears for any noise.

Suddenly, three guys in black leap out from behind a wall that's untouched by the destruction. Were they there the entire time?

"Travis!" one of them barks, his gloved hand hovering over a dagger at his belt.

We all turn to Travis. He smirks, but he looks a little confused.

"Which one has the stone?" the guy yells.

To my surprise and dismay, Travis fades through the ropes, passing through them as though they don't exist. They drop to the ground. Travis cracks his neck and stares at us, and I see a split second of hesitation on his face. In that moment, with all of us frozen in shock or fear, his eyes drop to my pocket, and I know he knows I have the stone.

51

Then, as though that second never happened, Travis grabs Nico by the shoulder and sends him sprawling over to the Evils. I cry out in protest and sprint after him, but Nora grabs my arm hard, yanking me back. He squirms in their grasp and shouts. I scream at Nora and try to kick at her, but she doesn't let go. As I shout, one Evil pulls out a black L-shaped device and points one end at my brother's head.

"Nobody move," Guy One says.

My heart skips a beat and I stop struggling, terrified for my brother.

Travis gives them a confident nod. "I'll finish these ones off."

The Evils nod back, hauling Nico like an inconvenient sack of potatoes. "The boss is mad that they got so far. We have to hurry back, but we'll come back for you."

They run off, and I manage to twist out of Nora's grip and try to dash after them. I run faster than I've ever run before, over the cracked pavement and broken glass that catches the light of the moon. I'm vaguely aware of the pounding footsteps of everyone else behind me.

"Jack!" Nico screams.

Every thought that I've ever had about not wanting to be responsible for my brother crashes down on me, weighing me down like a ton of scrap metal. I was too selfish, and now when he needs me the most, I can't do anything.

Nora catches up to me and clutches my arm again, holding me back. She grabs Thomas and hisses, "If you go over there, they'll kill both of you *and* your brother."

Cali glances at us, hearing Nora's words, and Thomas stands still. As the Evils run, Travis takes a small device out of his pocket, waits until the Evils are out of sight, and throws it at the wall.

"No! There has to be another way!"

I argue with Nora, despite what she said, until the device on the wall flashes red and beeps. The wall and connected building explode, dashing any hopes of going that way. Nora lets me and Thomas go, and I scramble up to the wreckage blocking the path. I try to get over it, but it's too high and unstable.

I finally give up and stare at the roadblock. I can't pursue them. I clench my teeth. It's like a piece of me has died on the inside. All my failures whisper in my ear, slowly tearing down my heart.

Thomas breaks the silence and shoves Travis, who hasn't moved from his position. "Why did you do that?" Thomas barks.

Nora gives me a sympathetic look. She turns to Travis and sighs, "Thanks."

I stagger away from them. The Evils have my brother. Why is she *thanking* him?

I spin around to face Nora. "How is this okay? They got my *brother*. And there's no way to get back to them! Where are they, anyway?"

My hands are shaking with rage. I want to scream at them, to scream forever.

"Don't you see?" Nora says. "He lied to them and cut off our path. By telling them your brother has the stone and exploding that wall, he's giving us time to get out of the city. If we go back to the Evils at your camp, we'll be overpowered, and any chance of escape or survival will be lost. We can't let Nico's kidnapping go in vain."

"I know you're upset," Travis mutters, "but please keep it to yourself. You're not the only person to ever lose someone. Besides, that stone is more important than any of us here. You can't give it to them."

Looking at Travis, I realize that I was once again broadcasting my emotions. As if it can't get any worse. I nod slowly. I want to understand, but I don't. You don't give up your family. Not even for a rock. Especially not for a rock. How can they possibly expect me to be okay with this?

I glare at him, like that will help get my brother back. I don't care what he says—to me, Nico is worth more than a million stones. But standing here, I'm helpless.

Nora waves her hand, motioning for us to follow. "I have a new plan. We get out of this city, find a new Good team. There should be a few around. At least that I remember."

Of course she has a plan. I survey the rubble separating me from Nico, wanting so badly to go after him. There's no telling what the Evils might do to him. But I know Nora is right. It's best we seek help.

When Travis follows Nora as well, I say to him, "Why are you coming? Your team is back there."

He rolls his eyes, not bothering to answer, as if I just asked the dumbest question ever uttered.

We walk in silence by the light of the moon for a few minutes. Strange noises coming from the darkest alleys make us flinch. A faint creaking sound grows, rising to a roar. Suddenly, a large shape shoots around the corner, barreling straight at us.

"Scatter!" Nora shouts.

We scramble toward the alley walls, trying not to get run over by whatever it is. I find myself pressed up against a building next to Travis and Cali.

"What the heck was that thing?" Cali hisses.

Travis's cold eyes narrow, sparkling in the dark. "I think that's our ride out of here."

"What?"

He doesn't answer. We watch as the shape turns and clambers toward us, following our voices. Cali balls her fists, but she appears to be nervous. The strange creature is coming closer.

A beam of moonlight hits the shape, illuminating its strange features. It appears to be completely made of metal. It walks on four huge, segmented spikes—legs in the shape of needles with joints connecting to the body. They're about six feet tall up to the mechanical joint and as thick as an adult human's leg. They look like spider legs, which is okay by me; I have nothing against spiders. The body is an oddly shaped hunk of metal, dented in several areas. It's sort of rectangular, with red spotlight eyes on one side that glare down at us. The creature stretches up to around ten feet tall, towering over us. The metal shines bronze, and the creature whirs and creaks.

This must be what we're warned about—what roams the city at night. My stomach tries to climb up into my throat, and my heart pounds. The creature lifts one of its legs, preparing to impale us, when Travis rushes forward and waves a shiny object.

"Kappa!" he shouts.

The metal creature pauses, its leg still in the air. Its red eyes narrow on Travis, shining scarlet lasers on his chest.

Cali and I slowly sidle away from the scene, hoping to be spared.

"Kappa, I am Travis Knight, Captain under specific orders to retrieve a special object in this area. Stand down." Travis's voice is calm and steady.

"Travis, what are you doing?" Nora hollers at him.

"Shut up!"

The creature tilts its rectangular body in apparent confusion and makes a few clicking noises. Just when I think it's backed down, faster than the speed of light, the creature pounds its leg straight through Travis, cracking the pavement behind him. Cali yelps, and Nora shrieks.

Travis's body shimmers, and he sighs and backs up, passing through the creature's leg, which was meant to kill him.

"Kappa, I order you to stand down," Travis commands.

The creature backs up, hissing. It tilts again, more dramatically than before, and falls over, revealing a smoking dent in its side. The metal screeches against the pavement, and the gears in the creature's legs creak.

Nora and Thomas jog over to us. We form a circle around the huge robotic beast.

"What is that?" Thomas asks.

"This is Kappa, a project released by the Evils," Travis explains. "She's a scout for the teams, but something must have happened to her. I was hoping she'd recognize my badge and follow my orders, but I suppose not."

"So it's a 'she' now, huh?" I muse. "This *thing* tried to kill you."

He frowns. "Oh well."

"Oh well?"

"Hey, wait," Thomas says. "Why were you trying to give it orders?"

"We can—"

"—ride it!" Nora exclaims, finishing Travis's sentence.

He gives her an annoyed look. "Not anymore."

"I might be able to fix it," Thomas says.

We all turn to Thomas, and he stares back at us.

"Well," Travis mutters, "go ahead."

Thomas places his hands on Kappa, stroking the dents and murmuring to himself as we watch. He knocks on the hunk of metal, and a panel pops open, exposing circuits and switches. Thomas fiddles with a few wires, and the creature begins to hum. We all back away as Kappa pounds her legs into the ground and rises. Her eyes now shine white instead of red, and she faces Thomas.

He smiles. "I think it's all good now."

"I didn't know you could do that," I tell him, amazed.

"Well, Kappa is a machine. I just did what felt right."

"Good job," Nora tells him. "What's your name? I don't think I caught it. I'm Nora."

"Thomas," he says sheepishly.

"Kappa," the robot whirs.

"Right," Travis says. "Thomas, tell Kappa to take us out of the city."

"Why me?" he asks, staring up at the metal creature with uncertainty.

"She acknowledged you first. She should be taking orders from you now," Travis explains, a hint of disappointment in his voice.

Thomas nods and clears his throat. "Kappa, we need a ride out of this city."

"West," Nora interjects. "Good teams settle in the west."

"Uh, we're heading west," Thomas says.

Kappa makes a couple of clicking noises. Her legs bend at the joints as she lowers herself to the ground so we can all climb on.

"Is there enough room for all of us?" Cali asks quietly, this being the first thing she's said in a while.

Nora grabs one of Kappa's legs, using it as a boost to climb up on the somewhat flat surface. Travis helps Cali and Thomas climb up next to Nora. When it's my turn, he climbs onto one of Kappa's legs and lends me a hand, pulling me up next to him. His grip is firm, and his hand is rough.

"If this thing goes really fast," Thomas says, "then won't we fall off with no seats or anything to hold on to?"

Travis blinks. "Ask Kappa for handles."

"Kappa, we need handles."

The metal under us shifts and molds into seats, and horizontal bars pop up in front of each of us. I grab my handle cautiously, though I'm sure Thomas knows what he's doing.

"We're ready," Thomas says, his voice growing more confident. "Let's go."

Chapter XI

Touch the Stars

The sun peeks over the horizon and the moon fades away. The shadows rise as dawn approaches. Cali and Thomas gape at the sunrise, their eyes sparkling in amazement. Even in this dull city, the sunrise is something special. Regret churns in my stomach as I find myself wishing Nico were here to experience it with us.

Kappa zooms through the streets, her legs covering more ground in minutes than we could on foot in hours. The ride is bumpy and nerve-wracking, and I clench the handle so hard my knuckles turn white. As we near the city wall—what's left of it, anyway—I expect Kappa to find a gate or exit. Instead, she digs her sharp legs into the wall and runs up vertically. We scream as we bound up and over, and out of the city.

The little dirt path we traverse is lined with shrubs and dry grass. I begin to sweat as the sun slowly crawls up the sky. It's ten times hotter outside the city. I wonder if this is what summer should be like. I wipe beads of perspiration off my forehead with one hand, gripping the handle with the other. It feels weird being out in the colorful open, away from the gray of the city and the shelter and shadows of the buildings and walls.

"I thought Evils didn't have abilities," Cali comments randomly.

I flash back to when Travis faded through the ropes, and when Kappa's leg went through him like he wasn't there.

"And why wouldn't they?" Travis asks, an edge in his voice.

"Because they're too evil."

I look over at her to see if she's serious. Thomas sighs.

Travis scoffs. "Not everyone is born with abilities. And you're completely wrong. Most Evils are born without them because their parents weren't exposed to chemically or radioactively charged weaponry that caused strange new modifications in humans, empowering them with inherent supernatural abilities. We don't give ourselves these abilities because the exposure to the radiation is hazardous and deadly, and the odds of survival are slim. The use of these weapons resulted in the Evil side having more people than any other side, though the power is balanced out with the rest of the world having powers—"

"Okay, that's too complicated. Never mind I asked."

I blink. It's as if he recited it from a textbook or something.

Thomas coughs into his hand. "Well, you have an ability. Or do all Evils pass through solid objects at will?"

When Travis doesn't answer, Nora says softly, "Some people switch sides."

Travis glares at her but doesn't elaborate. We ride in silence again until my stomach chooses a nice little moment to growl.

Cali giggles, and I whine, "Well, I haven't eaten since yesterday, so cut me some slack."

61

Travis fixes his cold indigo eyes on me. "You're lucky that you eat at all. In my team, if you don't get your own food, you starve."

Of course he had to say something.

I stare at the blueness of the sky. It seems unreal, since the only thing I remember since I was little is the gray tones of the sky in the city. I'm starting to relax, just enjoying the view, when all at once the fluffy white clouds take on a darker, almost red color. I blink and rub my eyes, wondering if I'm hallucinating.

A giant spark lands on my knee. It burns like fire. I yelp, my knee sizzling.

Nora's eyes widen and Travis hisses, "Flamestorm."

"Kappa, move! Find shelter!" Thomas cries as the fiery droplets rain down.

Kappa races across the rocky terrain, her metal skin smoldering where the droplets land. The smell of scorched cloth and metal rises, and little holes pepper our clothing. We reach a strange rock formation, and Kappa scrambles underneath. The rock arcs over our heads, shielding us from the fire. Kappa folds her legs under her and lowers us to the ground.

"What's going on?" I ask.

Nora stands up and scans the group, making sure we're all okay.

"Flamestorm," she explains. "I suspect it's a defense against people, which explains why the environment isn't burning. I'm not sure who or what's causing it, though one reason my team took shelter in your city was to get away from it."

"Probably the Evils are causing it," Thomas says as he stretches.

Cali rubs a burn on her arm. "Why would the Evils do this?"

I wrinkle my nose and respond before Travis or Nora can. "Because they're *evil*, duh."

Travis rolls his eyes but remains silent. He hops to the ground.

Standing, I lean to the side, my back popping. I shed my ruined coat and examine a few scorch marks on my arm.

"The stone, Jack. I heard it can heal," Nora says, glancing at my arm.

I take out the stone in all its glowing glory, holding it cautiously in case it tries to burn me or turn into a knife.

Travis looks annoyed. "The stone isn't some kind of medicine. It's an ability enhancer," he informs us.

"How do you know?" Nora mutters, glaring at him with her gray eyes.

He crosses his legs and replies, "Why would the Evils be searching for something they don't know about? The stone was made by a scientist that one of the teams captured, who was originally on a Good team. It's like a power-up."

"But why take it when the majority of your side has no abilities?" I ask.

"Good question," he says. "I don't really know, but I assumed it was to keep it out of anyone else's hands."

Nora throws a pebble at him. "That's pretty selfish."

"It's strategic."

"But why's it so important?" I think about how we traded my brother to keep it out of the Evils' hands.

"Because it could decide the fate of the war—the fate of the world, perhaps," Travis says. "Its power could tip the scales and destroy everything you've ever known."

Silence. I guess that conversation is over.

I grab my canteen from my belt. Nora watches the rain from her perch on top of Kappa. Travis tosses Cali some bandages from his pocket to wrap one of her major burns with. Thomas fiddles with a small metal object that looks suspiciously like a spider.

"Anyone want unfiltered water?" I ask, hoping to break the tension that the quiet always brings.

"I'll have some," Thomas says.

"Me too," Cali adds.

"I'll pass," Travis says.

I hand the canteen around, and I take a swig when it comes back to me.

I gaze out at the balls of fire raining from the sky. They make fizzling sounds as they land on the rocks and the sparse grass. The sun glares down at us, burning its path across the red sky.

Nora gets up and declares, "We need to move if we want to make any progress in finding another team."

I tilt my head. "But what about the rain?"

Nora nods, glancing back at the falling sparks.

"Well, I'm not affected, thanks to my ability," Travis says.

"Good for you." I go, exhaling.

Cali jumps up, her eyes bright. "What if I used *my* ability to move the fire droplets away from us as we travel?"

Nora claps for her and Travis whistles, but Thomas and I exchange worried glances.

"Can you even control fire? It's not a solid object," Thomas points out.

Cali grumbles something unintelligible and moves her hand to the edge of our shelter. My horror turns to awe when the little fire droplets dance around her palm and fingers, not touching her.

She gives Thomas a smug look. "Happy now?"

Thomas only sighs, and I mumble in agreement. What we're dealing with is dangerous, and I'm not as sure of Cali's ability as everyone else is.

Nora notices my expression. Or maybe I'm broadcasting.

"Have faith," she says.

We climb back on Kappa. Thomas knocks on her leg, telling her to wake up. Kappa slowly rises, then faces west. Cali lifts her arms before we head out from under the arch and into the rain.

If it weren't for the situation I'm in, with a missing brother and half the world trying to get me, I'd say the experience is rather fantastic. It's like we're in another world, just the five of us, traveling through a forgotten land on a mystical metal creature with an endless road in front of us. Where the stars aren't only in the sky, but all around us, close enough to touch.

It's surreal.

It's as though we can go on forever in this dreamlike moment, forget about our worries, and simply live life. The clouds turn several shades of scarlet, hiding the sun. Occasionally, sunlight filters through thin patches of cloud, shining on the celestial orbs raining around us and making them even more brilliant than before.

I want to live in this fantasy for the rest of my life, but all stories come to an end. And in a broken world like ours, those stories never end well.

Chapter XII

Snake

The fiery rain stops just as the sun reaches its highest point in the day. It blazes, making my exposed skin itch. As we venture through this area, the heat gets progressively worse. The metal we're sitting on goes from mildly warm to scalding, and soon enough we have to climb off of Kappa. The city has vanished in the distance, and all I can see for miles are thin chartreuse trees and shrubs, and rock formations.

We walk alongside Kappa, who has slowed to a human's regular walking pace. My canteen is empty now, so I hope we find someone soon.

Thomas squints at Kappa and says softly, "I don't know if she'll make it."

At first, the idea of referring to the robot as a girl with a name was strange, but after these past few hours, we've all become attached to Kappa, Thomas especially.

"Ask her if there's any way she can cool herself or save energy," Travis suggests.

Thomas pats Kappa's leg, despite it probably being hotter than a pot on a stove. "Hey, Kappa, if you have a way to cool down or save power, please do that."

The metal creature makes a few beeping noises, staring at Thomas with her big spotlight eyes. She makes a humming sound, and her legs fold together and into her body, which compacts to the approximate size of a packing box.

"That's going to be hard to take with us," Nora says gently. "Maybe we should leave her—"

"*No*," Thomas growls.

Nora gazes at him sadly, then sighs. "Okay."

I turn to Cali. "Would you be willing to use your ability on her?"

She slumps her shoulders. "I just tried, but I'm too tired. She's really heavy. I wouldn't even be able to lift you, Jack."

"It's fine," Thomas says. "I can do it myself."

We watch as he loops some rope around a handle on top of the block that is now Kappa.

"Make wheels," he tells the block.

Little wheels form under the block. Thomas slings the rope over his shoulder and pulls Kappa over the gravelly terrain.

As the sun moves across the sky, we continue to walk in the horrid heat, stopping every now and then to rest. We've been trudging through these ridiculous conditions for an eternity, and we still haven't found anyone. We pick up the pace, but I know no matter how fast we walk, we won't be able to escape our impending starvation and thirst and this heat.

"Well, thank you, Jack, for that," Nora mutters.

I kick a rock in annoyance. One of my biggest wishes is to be able to live without the fear of everyone knowing my thoughts.

"Don't worry," she says. "We've been heading west, and I know someone is out here."

A faint hissing sound erupts somewhere to our right, though in this heat I wonder if I imagined it. Then another one sounds, louder this time. Thomas and I stop in our tracks. By his rigid outline, I can tell he's terrified too.

I hold my breath and wait for the noise again. It feels like forever. When the hissing noise sounds again, it's accompanied by a rattle.

I flash back to four years ago, back at camp. Thomas and I were in the Long Room playing with these pieces of metal that he drew smiley faces on. Nicholas was four, still in the nursery with kids his age, so Thomas and I shared a bunk. We were sitting on the lower bunk, making our little metal figures swordfight with toothpicks from dinner, when suddenly Thomas screamed so loud that it sent a shock up my spine.

He was staring at something behind me, an expression of absolute terror on his face. I slowly turned my head to find a dark, scaly creature studying me. That day, I knew I had stared evil straight in the face.

It flicked a tiny forked tongue out at me and made a *sssss* sound. I stifled a yelp as an older kid appeared behind it with an iron pan and smacked the reptile to death.

That experience alone was enough to traumatize two young kids.

Cali looks over, her bright hair plastered to her forehead, and says, "What's wrong?"

Thomas doesn't respond—he's probably afraid to make any noise. I don't want to leave Cali hanging.

I focus on broadcasting only to the group, sending out, *"Snake nearby. Don't make a noise. Scary. Let's get away. Bad, bad."*

69

Not my most elaborate message, but I'm panicked. I need to tell them as fast as possible.

Cali picks up the message and sends back, *"Okay, so?"*

I'm happy she uses the thread to respond. But she doesn't sound scared. I repeat the message, and she answers with the same question. This goes on for a minute with a few irritated glares from Travis. He's not familiar with MindSpeak messages though, so I don't blame him for being mute.

Thomas finally gives his input in the thread. *"We don't like snakes. Bad history. Shut up, both of you. It's loud. We need to go."*

I frown at his explanation, but he's right. We do need to go. Cali stops repeating the question, so I suppose the matter is resolved.

I flinch when Nora appears beside me and whispers, "Jack, can you please not *think* at us? It's distracting. Besides, the snake won't do much since we're a group bigger than it. It's probably just warning us that it's there."

I guess her reasoning is correct. I nod and take a step forward.

"I don't think that's a snake, though," Travis mutters. "At least, that type of snake shouldn't be in these parts."

What does that mean? And what does he know? Nobody acknowledges his comment.

We move along quickly now, since Travis seems freaked as well. Nora walks behind the group, guarding us.

Every noise makes me jump, and I get the prickling sensation that we're being watched.

Another sound echoes over the open ground, giving me goose bumps despite the heat. It's a hooting noise, similar the one that owls make in the city. But it sounds off.

Travis hisses, "I knew it. *They're* here."

I almost ask what he's talking about when two more hisses answer. I close my mouth.

Travis grabs my collar and pushes me toward Cali and Thomas, so we're in a tight group. Nora backs up next to us, and Travis circles the formation protectively. Something's up, bad enough for him to stop us. By the way he's acting, it's worse than a couple of animals.

I don't mind—the extra protection is great—but Cali is frustrated. "You're crowding me! Travis, why'd we stop moving?"

He shushes her.

Travis lights a match, though in this heat and at this time of day I don't know what he could possibly need it for. I slip my hands into my pockets and close my fist around the stone, remembering its soft reassuring light, so unlike the scorching sun. The stone feels molded to my hand. Did I break it again? It had better not turn into a knife …

Taking on a strange loop shape in my hand, it wraps around my wrist and stops re-forming.

I take my hand out of my pocket. On my wrist is a glowing bracelet. At least now it looks a little bit more casual, minus the glowing part. It fits comfortably, but it doesn't seem like it'll come off.

Travis takes a step forward, his head cocked to the side, holding the match as if it's a dangerous weapon.

Nora starts to say something, but Travis cuts her off. He thrusts out the match, letting the small flame fly. The light sails to the right, and even though it rockets through the dry air, it doesn't flicker out.

My brain can't follow what my eyes are seeing. Everything happens so fast. The match lands, hitting something hidden behind a couple of tall rocks.

The something yelps, and a series of shrieks follow.

Chapter XIII

Warm Welcome

The screams keep on coming. I can't see Travis's face with his back turned to me, but I can see a figure off to our left flailing around, engulfed in flames. The light is bright and unnatural, and the smell of charcoal and sulfur rises.

How?

A match that small flying at such speed has no chance at lighting a moving target like that, unless it's covered in a flammable substance from head to toe. Even then, the possibility shouldn't be considered.

The figure keeps screeching, and I wince at each cry. We all stand, frozen, and watch, helpless and unsure of what's going on.

Nora hisses, "What have you done?"

Travis whips out another match and sets it ablaze. A few shouts ring out, and suddenly a horde of people appear. Cleverly camouflaged adults step out from behind shrubs and rock formations. Above us, people drop out of strange machines in the sky. They float down, huge circular cloths lowering them to the ground. People run in from behind us, and soon, we're surrounded and outnumbered. The person who was screaming is being carried away, no longer on fire.

After seeing one of their own attacked by the strange fire, the strangers stand still. A lady all in gray emerges from the wall of people and faces us.

She's older than Travis and Nora, maybe in her mid- to late twenties. Her strawberry-blond hair bounces around her shoulders. Her skin is fair, and her deep blue eyes are so intense that it's like a fire burns within them.

She stalks closer to us, unafraid of Travis's threat.

"Blow out your little candle or else there *will* be consequences," she declares.

"Do what she says, Travis," Nora whispers.

Travis lifts his chin, obviously not wanting to back down. But five seconds later, he takes a small cloth out of his pocket and smothers the tiny flame with it.

"Now, get on your knees with your hands on your head," she instructs.

"Excuse me?" Cali puts her hands on her hips, not buying it.

"We don't mean you any harm," Nora tries. "We're just looking for a team that can help us."

"Get on your knees with your hands on your head," the lady repeats, crossing her arms.

"Why?" I ask impatiently, not wanting to stand in the heat any longer. I'm tired of this weather, of my situation, of this world. In general, I'm just really tired.

Thomas stands at my shoulder, crossing his arms too, giving the strangers his best glare. I do the same, despite how intimidating the larger group is. The lady only stares at us, her blue eyes reflecting the sun.

Nora sighs, "Okay."

"What?" Travis cries. "We don't have *time* for this!"

"I'm sure you can spare a little time," the lady says. "You're obviously exhausted and weak. You won't be able to hold off all of my soldiers. Stand down, and no one will be hurt."

The lady flashes a weapon much like the device the Evils had. Nora nods at me. I drop to my knees and raise my hands, placing them on my head, feeling kind of stupid. Cali and Thomas follow my example, then Nora drops down, leaving Travis standing.

"What are you doing?!" Travis hisses. "This obviously isn't a Good team!"

"*Travis.*"

Travis drops down on his knees.

I focus my eyes on the ground as the lady barks a word and the strangers surge forward, clamping cuffs on our wrists.

A man yanks me to my feet; other adults grab my friends. Thomas shouts at a couple of people who lift Kappa, but they ignore him.

The man pushes me along, muttering, "This ain't no ordinary place yer visitin', kid."

I don't try to fight him. The lady was right—I'm too exhausted from walking around with no food or water. I hope Nora has a plan, considering she always has an answer for everything. She wouldn't back down that easily if she wasn't up to something, would she?

I hope these people will have mercy on us.

They lead us to a giant building that stretches up at least forty floors, excessively topped with a dome. The walk took about as long as dinner back at camp, so how we

75

never noticed it, I have no idea. It just seems to appear here. The building rests on cracked ground with minimal shrubs and barely any grass. It's the exact description of a desert, though it lacks the mythical spikey barrels known as cacti. Next to the building are water towers with dark letters on the side that I can't make out.

We enter the building. The lobby has chairs and benches lining the walls, and doors and hallways leading away from the main section. The walls are light gray, and the floor is a darker shade of tile. A comfortable pocket of nice, cool air blankets me.

We go up to the wall opposite from where we entered. It's blank except for two metal doors awaiting us. One of our captors presses a button next to the door on the right, and it slides away, revealing a room that's no bigger than a medium-sized closet.

The lady and her fellow kidnappers force us into the box. The ones holding us step in after us. The rest of the group disperses. The man who put the cuffs on me pushes a button inside the box-closet. A group of people drag Kappa away as the metal doors close.

I glance around nervously, feeling claustrophobic from being crowded in the tight space with a bunch of other people. My breathing quickens. I can't get enough air, and my hands are cold and clammy. The box hums a little, and it jolts slightly, which doesn't help calm my nerves.

Nora gives me a reassuring smile. She looks almost confident.

I glance at Cali, then Thomas, but they're each focused on something—the floor, the wooden wall. The box shudders, then drops, leaving my stomach behind on the first floor. The sensation of falling gives me a momentary sense of weightlessness. In this moment, I understand Nico's fear of heights. The box stops abruptly, almost sending me to the floor. It shakes again, now pulling us downward at a slower pace.

I don't dare peek at our captors, so I force myself to stare at Travis. Our eyes meet. He gives me a tight smile, but the rest of his face shows anything but consolation. He looks like he's already come to terms with our fate. I quickly shift my eyes to my boots.

The box finally shudders to a stop. The doors open.

We're shoved out into a dim hallway, much unlike the bright light outside. Colorful spots dance over my vision, and I blink a few times to let my eyes adjust. A lady with bright green hair leads Cali and Nora into a room at the very end of the hallway. The man guides Thomas, Travis, and I to another, leaving the other three adults waiting at the box entrance.

The man pushes us into the room and locks the door behind him, then he pulls out a small gun-shaped device. Travis turns and lunges at him, but the man pulls the trigger and a tiny pin shoots out. It goes through Travis's scarf and embeds itself in his neck.

I gasp as Travis falls. A second later, he's snoring. Thomas looks up, his eyes wide, as another dart flies through the air. He crumples into a ball on the floor. I step away from the man, in shock, as he aims his gun at me. A cold wave creeps over me, and my stomach sinks.

"Welcome to the Indifferents," he says.

The last thing I see is the floor before everything goes black.

Chapter XIV

Wake Up

A series of images pass through my mind: Nico speaking urgently to someone, a sharp piece of metal being fired from a gun, a stray dog I saw on one of my trips to get supplies.

They go by in one big *whoosh*.

The darkness fades and I can see, even though I don't open my eyes. It's the same feeling I had when the stone separated my mind from my body back at camp, putting me into a ghost-like state. Everything is dim and fuzzy, and outlined with the same aqua color as the stone.

I see my body, glowing brightly, limp on the floor. Thomas is there as well, his light a little duller than mine, but still bright enough that I have to blink away the spots.

Just in front of Thomas is Travis. Instead of aqua, his light is scarlet. It's blinding. I look away.

It's weird—I'm in the air, suspended in time, unable to fall. Like gravity doesn't exist. I float a little higher, almost to the ceiling, and I lean forward to move.

My mind is filled with a chaotic static buzz, and a million currents are tugging me in all directions, begging me to follow. I remind myself that I have all the control in this state, that this is *my* mind space. Leaving my body behind, I drift toward the exit. I pass through the door, and suddenly I'm in the hallway. This must be how Travis feels when he uses his ability. Like he's made of air.

I think back to that scarlet color and how vastly different it is from ours. What could possibly make the stone perceive him in a completely different color?

I glide down the hall to the room I saw Nora and Cali go into. I pass through the door; they're there, sleeping on the floor. Cali's light is strong, the same as before, and Nora's is about the same brightness as mine.

Reaching out with my nonexistent hand to tap Nora's shoulder, I'm suddenly in a whole other world.

I'm not a floaty thing anymore—just regular me, standing in the middle of a circle of kids. They're playing a word game with a brightly colored ball, but none of the words make sense. They toss the ball around the circle, shouting as they receive it.

"Zebra!"

"Baguette!"

"Floral design!"

"Drama!"

The list goes on and on. I spot a kid who resembles Nora, with the same gray eyes and bandana. I realize it *is* Nora, only younger. When I walk in front of her, she looks past me like I'm not there. I wave my hand in her face, but she doesn't react. She keeps smiling, waiting for her turn.

Just behind the group sits another kid, his knees up to his chin, his indigo-colored eyes full of boredom and maybe even melancholy. His dusty-brown hair and pale complexion are familiar. Then it hits me. Travis! He looks up, stares directly at me, and smiles.

The circle of kids disappears. Their brightly colored ball flies over my head, and next I'm standing in a large tent. There's a desk at the back and three sleeping bags on the ground. A younger Nora and Travis are discussing something. Travis waves his hands around like he's trying to shape the words he's saying.

"It's too dangerous! If we go tomorrow, we have a better chance at succeeding in the skirmish. There's no point in endangering ourselves," he says.

"I know what I saw," Nora interjects. "We'll be fine if we go tonight. The team has already decided."

"It's idiotic," Travis mutters, then his eyes light up as if he has an idea. He starts to say something, waving his arm, and the scene changes again.

Fire blazes through a grassy field. I levitate at a bird's eye view, looking down on a raging battle. I spot Nora wielding a shimmering sword, fighting two people twice her size. Behind her, Travis kneels on the ground, cradling a woman with dusty-brown hair and intelligent eyes. She coughs and reaches up to touch Travis's face. Her hand falls short and drops to the ground. I realize with a shaky breath that the woman is dead.

Travis stands up, his shoulders rigid. He can't be much older than I am now. His indigo eyes full of grief and something else, he runs away from Nora and the dead woman. A nearby wooden structure falls and the burning wood tumbles to the ground over him. He glances up as it makes its impact. A piece of the burning wood hits Travis in the face. He shimmers and runs through the wreckage and away from the battle.

Nora turns to him and shouts, but he's already gone.

The scene fades, crumbling around me like dust.

I'm back in Nora and Cali's room, back to my old floaty self. Yay for floatiness.

What was that? A dream? A memory? Somehow, I'm able to go into other people's minds. It's MindSpeak but on a completely different level.

The stone isn't some kind of medicine, it's an ability enhancer, whispers a slightly annoyed voice in my mind.

An ability enhancer. That's how I'm being Supreme Master Floaty, and how I'm able to access Nora's thoughts and memories. It's the stone!

I need to get back to my body. Quickly. It would be fun to let the currents pull me around, to explore everyone's minds, but a small part of me nags at the thought of trespassing on them.

It's not like they'll know. Who cares? says another thought.

No, not now. I have priorities. My friends come first.

I float back to the room where my body lies. As I approach, I notice I'm face-planted in a very awkward and unflattering position. I reach my thoughts back to my body, and everything is back to normal. I'm awake.

I sit up.

No more fuzziness or floating. No flashes of blinding light. No more memories.

I try to get up, but my hands are still cuffed. How irritating. I struggle up to my knees and then my feet. My leg no longer hurts, which I take as a good sign. I take in my surroundings. The room is relatively small, with light

81

gray walls and no furniture or carpet. We couldn't have been asleep for too long since I still feel exhausted.

I stomp over to Thomas, trying to wake up my numb feet. I nudge him with my boot.

"Hey, Thomas," I call.

He groans but doesn't budge. I sigh and stumble over to Travis.

I kick him and jump back when he leaps up as fast as a snake, his face tensed. Maybe I shouldn't have kicked him.

He lunges toward me blindly, and I fall back on my behind, shocked that he's moving around and attacking me so soon after being in a deep sleep.

"Hey, hey, hey!" I yell, scared he might strangle me even though his hands are tied behind his back, too.

He blinks and stares at me with a startled, savage expression. I gaze up at him. By his unimpressed reaction, I'm guessing I look as pathetic and terrified as I feel.

"You know, you don't have to attack everyone who tries to wake you up. I was just trying to help," I say, squaring my shoulders and trying to appear tough.

He looks at me, not saying anything, as if he's lost in thought.

With a shrug, I add, "Is this what you would do to your mom every time she'd wake you up?"

That seems to strike a nerve. His glare is fearsome, shadows mark his face, his scar stands out in the light like a fresh wound, like he's just been struck in the face with the burning piece of wood.

I gulp as he says in a tone that's deadly serious, "My parents are dead. They've been dead."

That is enough to make a situation awkward. I turn away, unsure of how to respond, hoping he gets the signal that I'm not ready to talk to him anymore.

I crawl over to Thomas as best I can with my hands tied behind my back. I hear Travis moving behind me, then the hard *clank* of something dropping to the floor.

I'm about to stand up and kick Thomas, hoping he'll wake up with the same energy as Travis, when Travis crouches beside me, flexing his freed hands.

"I'm sorry about attacking you, Jack. I'm used to waking up to enemies. It was just an involuntary action."

I nod and mumble, "I'm sorry about your parents."

He shrugs. "I've gone this long without them."

I kick Thomas with a little more force than I used to wake up Travis. He mutters something unintelligible and sits up groggily.

Smiling at him, I turn around so he can see my wrists. "Can you undo them?"

He gives me a, "Meh."

I guess he can.

Another *clank* sounds, then Thomas's rough fingers are working magic on my bindings. I find it a little unfair that I'm the one who woke up first and gets freed last.

The chafing bands drop from my hands with their own satisfying *clank*. I rub my wrists. My stone-bracelet is still there.

Behind me, Travis curses. "They took my matches."

I chuckle, despite the severity of our situation.

"I'm just glad they didn't take the stone," I say, showing him the bracelet. He nods.

"They took Kappa, too," Thomas says, his voice barely masking his anger.

"We'll find her," I assure him. "Once we figure out how to get out of here."

I stretch, popping some joints in my back. Thomas follows my example, rolling his shoulders and cracking his knuckles. Travis leans against the wall and takes off his boot. I bite back a comment about letting us smell his feet and watch as he pulls a tiny rectangular box out of a pocket on the inside of his boot.

He unfolds it until it's as long as my hand. But it's no longer a box—it's a small dagger. Of course. Just like him to keep a pocketknife in his boot.

Travis smirks at me and points his knife at the door.

Sure enough, someone's coming.

Chapter XV

Duel

I freeze. My heart skips a beat as the door unlocks. Luckily for us, Travis is next to the door with his knife in hand, so when it opens, he'll be behind it.

Travis hisses to us, "Put your hands behind your backs and sit down!"

Thomas obeys, but I hesitate. Why would we do that? But when the door starts to move, I follow Travis's instructions. If he has a plan, it's best to cooperate.

Holding my hands behind my back, I slide down the wall and sit cross-legged. Thomas sits in the middle of the room.

I try to hide my terror as the lady with the pale strawberry-blond hair walks in, holding one of the gun devices. Her blue eyes narrow with suspicion as if she's doing the math and realizing that there are only two of us.

Travis doesn't give her much time to think. He kicks the door in her face. She staggers back, but it only fazes her for a moment. With her weapon drawn, she leaps at Travis, her main threat. I jump to my feet, ready to help him, realizing at the last second that I might get in the way.

The lady points her weapon at Travis, but he grabs her wrist, pointing the device upward and knocking it out of her hand, all in one fluid motion.

My first impression is that he's strong, but as I watch the skirmish, I find the lady is stronger.

She twists around, yanks her hand away, shoulders him in the chest, and elbows him in the gut. The sudden force makes him step back, but he recovers quickly. He whips around with his pocketknife.

I watch the duel for a second, then I turn to Thomas for any ideas. By his shocked expression, I can tell he has no clue.

Travis dodges a kick just in time. He swipes at the lady's face, but she's too fast. She's going to win.

So I do the only thing that I can. With a weak battle cry, I tackle her.

My force combined with her shock is enough to knock her off her feet. She stumbles backward and slips, and we both crash to the floor. Even though she's way tougher than me, I manage to hold my ground. She pushes at me, and I try to fight, but my punches are slow, and I'm still dazed from the fall.

Out of the corner of my eye, I see Travis analyzing the situation. My main hope is that he doesn't try to attack the lady; I might be stabbed.

The lady flings me off, and I fly into the wall. Thomas rushes to my side. My head pounding, I sit up and wipe my nose. Blood.

"Are you okay?" Thomas asks, but it's muffled and sounds like, *"Aw hoo oh-ay?"*

"No, thank you," I manage.

His confused expression means I probably made no sense. I try to get up, but my vision blurs, and my shoulder throbs. I must have jarred it when I was thrown into the wall. I wince, but with Thomas's help, I get to my feet.

I glance up and flinch as the woman swings Travis into the opposite wall. I catch his eye, and in that second he mouths one word. "Go."

He's right. There's no choice. I grab Thomas's wrist and tug him out of the room and into the hallway. I close my eyes for a moment and think. She'll forget about Travis and come after us, knowing that we're free. I can't risk that, not even for Travis's sake.

I yank the handle of the door and close it. Thomas gets the idea. He presses his fingers to the door, locking it. I tilt my head, pointing my chin at where Nora and Cali are being held.

Thomas and I sprint down the hallway.

I catch my breath while Thomas picks the lock. The door swings open, and Nora and Cali look up in surprise.

They jump up off the floor and pepper us with questions.

"How'd you escape?"

"Did they let you out?"

"Are you okay?"

"Where's Travis?"

I hold up my hands, and they stop. As Thomas works on their cuffs, I launch into the story of what happened, with a few details about the stone. I tell them about the drifting bits, but I don't mention going into Nora's mind. They both nod, and Thomas raises his eyebrows at me, like, *How come you didn't say anything about the stone earlier?*

I smile sheepishly. *Whoops.*

A heavy *smack* echoes from down the hall. We all turn in the direction of the door when Travis tumbles through it, clutching the doorframe like his life depends on it. I nearly jump out of my skin, but try to remain cool, not wanting to show him that he scared me once again.

He looks like he just walked off a battlefield, with several bruises and a blood-stained cheek. Weirdest of all, his knuckles are charred. Travis takes off his ripped scarf and wipes his mouth, the source of the blood.

We all gawk at him for a moment. Nora breaks the silence. "What happened to you?"

"She ... the woman had this ability. Pyrokinesis. Very, very strong."

Cali, Thomas, and I stare at each other in confusion.

"She can create and control flames with her mind," Nora explains.

I nod, the fancy word lighting a spark in my mind, filling one little gap. Theories about the flamestorm and the lady bounce around my head.

Travis rips his scarf in two and wraps the pieces around his burned hands. Then, without a word, he turns and marches out. We follow with no hesitation. We need to stick together.

"I think we should look for Kappa first," Thomas says as we walk.

Nora nods. "I saw her being taken away. I do know we're underground, so we have to go up, but the number system here is weird."

We reach the box that carried us down here using buttons. Nora tells us that it's an elevator, and fancy buildings have them. Cali eagerly presses a button on the wall, which supposedly tells the elevator to come pick us up. As we wait, I wonder what's happening to our camp, and what's happened to Nico. I bite the inside of my lip, trying not to have a breakdown right then and there, thinking about all the horrible things that the Evils might do to my brother. I know I have to be strong for his sake, but the regret churning in my stomach makes me want to throw up.

If only my problems were as easy as elevators. One click of a button, a couple of minutes, and *whoosh*, they're solved. We step into the box and I frown at the multitude of buttons on the inside. Each, Nora tells us, are for a specific floor number. My problems aren't as solvable as an elevator, but they *are* actually as overwhelming as the number of buttons on the inside.

What will happen to Nico? Is he even ...?

No. I need to stop with the machine metaphors. I have to believe that our camp is still there. I have to believe that we can save it. We *will* make it back.

Chapter XVI

Reunion

We storm through the building, marching down corridors, despite our unfortunate state. Nora leads the way, with Travis watching our back. We try to get him to relax, but he refuses, saying he's just battered.

Yeah, right.

He gives me this scorching look, hotter than fire, and I know he hears my thoughts.

Whoops.

I can't remember the last time I broadcasted. Could this mean I'm starting to control my ability better?

After a few minutes of power walking through the corridors, a deep voice emits from the walls, where I assume loudspeakers are hidden.

"Attention, Indifferents. We have a breach of security. Five prisoners with dangerous capabilities have escaped. All range between the ages of twelve and sixteen. If seen, please report immediately. Engage and use force if necessary."

I flinch at the gruff voice demanding our recapture.

"Hey, Nora?" I say. "Can't you just turn us all invisible?"

Nora sighs. "Not all five of us at once, and not under these conditions, sorry."

"Oh."

We all pick up the pace, hoping to not encounter anyone. But that's not how it goes.

We spring around a corner and are immediately faced with two mean-looking soldiers. Both are dressed in light armor, and each have a sleep-gun. I manage to leap out of the firing line, but Nora's not as lucky.

Soldier One pulls the trigger and aims at Nora. I shout a warning, but the dart grazes her shoulder. She flicks it away but staggers back, almost falling over. Thomas catches her, and we all retreat around the corner.

I concentrate on opening a telepathic line with only my friends so that they can use it too, as long as I can hold it and don't get distracted.

"Any ideas? Don't talk out loud. We don't have much time before they investigate," I say.

Travis presses himself against the wall, ignoring me, but Thomas and Cali stare directly at me, probably still thinking. They'd better think fast, before I get too tired to hold the thread open.

"Throw something in the open to serve as a distraction," Thomas suggests. *"Maybe an ambush?"*

I nod. It's not the most original or foolproof idea, but it's all we have. Nora yawns and leans against the wall, blinking slowly. Her head tilts forward, and she closes her eyes. Oh, great. Cali takes off her boot, and I close the thread. It seems we all got the message.

Travis peeks around the corner, then holds out three fingers.

Three …

Cali puts the boot on the ground and holds her hand over it, like she's blessing it.

Two …

The footwear lifts off the ground. We all inch away from it like it's possessed, which I guess it kind of is.

One.

The boot zooms around the corner, and a confused shriek follows. A few darts are shot into the wall. Cali drops her hand, and I hear the boot drop with it.

Multiple hesitant footsteps grow closer as Nora slides down the wall, her eyes closed. Cali, Travis, Thomas, and I form a line just outside the sharp bend in the hallway.

When the two guards walk out, their weapons cocked, Travis lunges. He tackles one of them and the weapon skitters to the floor. He quickly uses that to his advantage and puts the sentry in a headlock.

Soldier Two steps away from us nervously. "Don't … Don't move! Or else!"

Cali chuckles. "Or else what?"

Soldier Two gulps, her hands shaking. I tilt my head, wondering why she's so scared of a bunch of kids.

Cali points her finger at Soldier Two. She levitates and turns in the direction of the wall so she can't aim her gun at us. I grab Nora's arm and help her up. She stumbles, half-asleep, and I grumble with frustration.

Travis takes a dart from Soldier One's weapon and sticks it in the man's neck. He slumps, fast asleep. Travis drops him and strides over to the floating guard. She curses at us, attempting in vain to struggle out of Cali's gravitational challenge by kicking her legs and waving her arms as if trying to swim.

"Where are you holding Kappa?" Thomas demands.

Soldier Two looks over her shoulder and eyes Thomas nervously. "Who?"

"Our robot," I say. "When you captured us, you took a metal box with wheels. Where did you put her?"

"On the e—eighth floor," Soldier Two stammers, beads of sweat trickling down the side of her face. "The box is in a storage r—room."

We all glance at each other.

"Thanks," I say.

"Can you let me go?" she asks.

"Nope," Cali answers.

"Lights out." Travis pricks Soldier Two.

Cali gently places the soldier down, and she curls up, snoring loudly. She grabs her boot and hurries down the hall after us, hopping into it as she goes.

Nora leans against Thomas, while Cali charges ahead of us. Travis walks beside me. He hands me one of the weapons he acquired from the guards.

I gaze at the small machine in my hands, considering the harm it can cause. With a shake of my head, I give it back. I can't use it.

Not can't—I know how it works. No, no, I *won't* use it. It only puts people to sleep, but it still bothers me. I can't wish that feeling of powerlessness on someone else, even if they are my enemy. I won't.

Travis doesn't understand. He frowns, his eyes full of disbelief at my refusal. "Why won't you take it?"

"Sometimes weapons can't solve your problems," I answer, staring at the scarf wrapped firmly around Travis's knuckles so I won't have to meet his eyes.

He sighs and shoulders past me with both guns. We continue our trek back to the elevator. Travis presses the button for Floor Eight, and after a few seconds, the doors open up to a corridor.

We walk through hallway after identical hallway. They all share the same gray walls and tile floor, with lights lining the ceiling. As we go, we open doors, searching for the storage room.

We peer around a corner. Three adults stand in front of a large door similar to the elevator doors. They each have guns at their belts.

"That's got to be it," Thomas whispers.

I nod.

Cali takes off both of her boots. "I'ma see if I can hit them in the head and knock them out. Then we'll only have one to deal with."

"Go for it," Travis says.

Cali makes the boots levitate off the ground and sends them zooming around the corner. I hear the harsh *crack* of flying footwear connecting with human noses and the *thud* of bodies falling to the floor. We peer around the corner again to see one very confused guard staring down at the other two.

The guard looks up just as Travis shoots him in the chest. He falls over on top of his comrade, snoring. We step over the bodies, and Thomas presses his hand to the padlock next to the door. The metal wall slides open, revealing rows and rows of shelves holding crates and miscellaneous items. The room is about as big as the Dining Hall, with bright lights on the ceiling and no windows.

Once we're all inside, Thomas closes the door behind us. He cups his hands around his mouth and shouts, "Kappa!"

No answer.

We leave Nora sitting at the door and split up to explore the huge room, to carefully scrutinize each shelf and pace through the aisles, looking for a metal box on wheels. It takes a long while of searching up and down rows of crates until Travis calls out that he found her.

We meet at Travis's location and lift Kappa off the shelf, then stand in a circle around the robot and examine the box. She appears shinier than before, and her dents are gone. Overall, it seems as though the Indifferents fixed Kappa up. Thomas checks the circuit panel and messes around with it, re-plugging wires. When he's finished, he motions for us to carry Kappa back to the entrance of the storage room before popping the panel back in place. She's heavy, but it doesn't take long for us to navigate back and set her down.

"Kappa," Thomas says.

The box roars to life. The metal shifts and folds as Kappa expands. But the transformation is different. Instead of four giant legs folding out from a rectangular body, four human-like limbs pop out from the box. A body stretches upward. After a minute, instead of a huge metal creature, a teenage girl of Nora's height, stands in front of us. We all stare at her, and Thomas's jaw hangs open.

Her features are smooth and shiny, but she's sturdy and tough. Her metallic skin is glistening bronze, and her hair is a darker shade of bronze coils braided down her back. She wears sheets of metal as a dress, and she's barefoot. She's almost a completely different creation, except when I look into her shining white eyes, I can tell it's the same Kappa.

"K—Kappa?" Thomas stutters.

"Yes, sir," she responds. Her voice contains an eerie lilt, almost like she's singing.

"I knew she could transform into various things," Travis says, "but I had no idea she could do *that*."

Kappa faces Travis. "Yes, Captain, you are correct. The engineers and inventors here fixed me up, repairing my human body in the process. Exciting, isn't it?"

He just stares at her.

"This is *amazing!*" Thomas practically shouts.

Kappa turns back to him, smiling warmly. Her smile is so human that I almost forget she's a robot.

"What shall we do now, sir?" she inquires in that lilting voice.

"Call me Thomas, please," Thomas says. "We need to find a Good team to help our camp."

"Yes, Thomas, sir," Kappa says cheerily.

We walk back to the door when the deep voice on the speakers buzzes again. "Attention, Indifferents. The prisoners have not been recaptured and contained.

96

Unauthorized people have been using the elevators. Indifferents, please report any suspicious activity to the main office."

Travis frowns. "We have to move. We can't use the elevator anymore, though."

"That's okay," Cali says. "I'm sure they have stairs."

We exit the storage room, Kappa carrying Nora with ease. She bounds ahead of us, her energy completely restored.

"Kappa, wait up!" Thomas calls.

Kappa turns around, smiling. "Yes, Thomas, sir."

We find the stairs, taking them two at a time. I'm starving, thirsty, and exhausted, but I manage to keep up with the group.

More and more hallways and staircases follow. We keep going, ignoring the occasional orders over the speakers and fighting the sentries stationed in corridors. Kappa does most of the fighting, though.

We eventually stop at a dead end after fighting off two more guards.

"Great, we're lost," Thomas grumbles. "We've *been* lost since we got here. Now what?"

"I'm sorry, Thomas, sir," Kappa says.

But something isn't right. Why would soldiers guard a hallway with a dead end? I squint at a pattern of cracks in the wall.

"Thomas, wait," I say. "Put your hand on the wall."

The moment his fingers connect with the bricks, his frustrated expression melts away. As he runs his fingers down the grooves in the wall, the bricks fold in on each other, rotating, sliding, moving, creating an opening. Behind the wall is a medium-sized room with a long rectangular table and a couple of desks. Maps and papers are plastered across the walls.

"Amazing job, Thomas, sir!" Kappa applauds.

Sitting at the table facing the left wall, a person with short, curly black hair gazes intently at a piece of worn, crinkled paper. I don't care about the kid, though. What matters to me are the people standing behind him.

One is a short lady with rusty-red hair, and I know if she turned around she'd have a mole below one of her emerald-green eyes. Beside her stands a man with tousled brown hair, an olive complexion, and eyes that glow gold and green.

I fight the urge to cry. Thomas and Cali gasp, and the trio turns to see who came in. The boy with the paper looks up with a friendly smile and goes back to his work, not seeming bothered by a bunch of intruders. But my parents ... my parents!

I break away from the group and run to them. My mother rushes to me first, embracing me with her gentle yet firm hug. My father wraps his arms around the both of us, lifting us off the ground for a second. We stand there, laughing.

"What are you doing here?" I ask with a grin.

"We stumbled into this place on a scouting mission," my mom says. She frowns. "*You're* outside of the city."

I smile and nod happily, too excited to care about rules.

Dad repeats her statement with a question. "What are you doing outside of the city?"

My grin fades as everything that happened in the past couple of days comes rushing back with a tidal wave of guilt. I look back at my friends. It would almost be perfect if Nico were here. Mom reads my mind, even though I'm not broadcasting.

"Where's Nicholas?" she asks, her voice rising with apprehension.

I don't want to meet anyone's eyes, especially not my mom's. The wall we came in through makes a convenient staring contest partner. It's closed, a smart move on Thomas's part.

Thomas waves to my dad and moves up next to me with Kappa loyally trailing behind him. Cali walks over to help me explain our situation to my parents. We recount the Evil invasion, how we met Kappa, and how we got captured by the Indifferents. My mother makes a strangled sound in the back of her throat when I tell her about Nico, like she's trying to hold back an anguished scream. I turn my head away, too ashamed and pained to look at her. It was hard enough for me to let Nico go, but he's her baby, and she loves him. My dad slumps his shoulders, but he seems to understand. I know he'd do anything for Nico, but he's a more optimistic person, and any chance my brother is okay will give him hope.

Nora is leaning against the wall, her eyes half-closed. Travis stands next to her, studying my parents with that calculating expression of his. His poker face is perfect, but his body language is a little less mysterious. His shoulders are rigid, and his head is slightly lowered.

My mom glares at him with the passion of a million suns. I tap her shoulder, telling her to go easy on him.

"There's nothing we could do," I explain. "It wasn't just his fault. We're all to blame. Besides, he helped us a lot, too."

My mom sighs, lowering her gaze.

Travis turns away, exhaling slowly. Knowing a bit of his past, I can't help but have sympathy for him. I can't know what he's going through, and that makes it difficult to get a hold on him.

Nora wakes up with full awareness, alarmed at the unfamiliar adults in the room. While Travis fills her in on the details, Mom asks us to join the other person in the room.

"We'd like to introduce you to someone," she says. Her voice still has a dangerous edge to it—she's really upset about Nico.

"This is Cole. He's this super-camp's scientist," Dad says, "even though he's around your age, Jack."

Cole smiles at me. "Hello, Jack Barret. I have heard much about you."

His voice is high pitched, reminding me of Nicholas, but the way he speaks is different. Not foreign, exactly, but sort of formal, or old. Like someone's grandparent. It doesn't make much sense, but that's all I can think of.

I nod and hold out my hand to shake his. He's wearing leathery red gloves that end at his knuckles. I nod again. Awkward.

Mom clears her throat. "These people are known as the Indifferents. As you probably know, indifferent means that they don't care about what's going on. But really, they're neutral. They're a giant camp, and they recruit smaller camps like ours. I'll see if I can convince Thala to help us."

I tilt my head. *Thala?*

"Thala is the lady you ran into on your journey," Dad says. "Good thing you did. She's the leader around here."

"Was she the one causing the flamestorm?" Travis asks, rubbing his thumb over his knuckles. "I've been through here before with both sides, and every time, it happens. The teams have come to call these areas the 'Land of Fire.' We'd known there was a super-camp around here, but we never suspected it to be the cause."

Mom frowns in Travis's direction. "Yes, Thala is quite powerful."

"Cole, can you please notify Thala to our position?" Dad says. "Oh, and ask her to not bring the entire army, please."

Cole nods and slides a large machine with glowing lights across the table and presses several buttons. He taps multiple times, each in a different but similar pattern.

"You know Morse?" Nora asks excitedly. "It's such an old technique of communicating that I thought I'd never find another who could do it."

"I know several other languages," Cole answers with a grin, "Morse has been my preferred use of communication, and fortunately, the Indifferents are fast learners. I've been using it for a while, really, to the point where I see dots and dashes in my head instead of regular characters."

Nora and Cole geek out for a while over "Morse code," whatever that means, until a bell rings. Cole stands up and walks over to the door. He pulls a switch and the bricks separate as they did before.

Outside stands the lady that Travis fought. The side of her face is patched with bandages.

I move next to Travis, hissing, "What did you do?"

He frowns and rubs the cloth wrapped firmly around his hand. "I'm not really sure," he whispers. "It was mostly a blur for me, but I'm pretty sure she ran her face into the wall at the end of the fight."

I decide not to question it.

Thala walks in, her strawberry-blond hair hanging loosely over her face. She brushes it away and appraises us coldly.

"I hear we have a problem with a group of unofficial Indifferents and an Evil team."

Chapter XVII

Plans and Secrets

We sit around a circular table. I fold my hands in front of me, trying to ignore my sore shoulder and my gradually growing hunger. My parents summarize the events we shared with them with Thala, who stares at me for a moment before prying her gaze away and clearing her throat.

Cole looks up from his paper. Nora watches Thala intently, not to miss any details. Next to me are Thomas and Cali. Their eyes are focused on the apple in a bowl at the center of the table. I watch the fruit too, wondering how long it's been since I've eaten.

"Let me get this straight," Thala begins.

I mean, the entire journey I've been hungry, but now it's starting to take its toll on me and my thinking. I sit forward in my seat, contemplating whether or not to grab the piece of fruit. So shiny ... So red ...

"Jack?" Thala calls.

"Yes?" My voice cracks as I jerk my head up.

Thala sighs and repeats herself. "Your parents tell me that a fairly large Evil team attacked your camp for a glowing stone?"

I nod. Anything to keep her talking, to get this meeting over with. I tap my wrist impatiently, staring at the wall.

"May I see it?" Thala asks.

I think she's talking to someone else, still reviewing everything that's happened while I think about the last time I ate. But she coughs loudly in my direction.

"The stone? Sure, just ... Um, hold on a second."

I shake my wrist, hoping the stone comes off and turns back into, well, a stone. After a few embarrassing minutes, I wish with all my might for the bracelet to melt off my wrist and morph into a rock. It does, and I slide it over to Thala.

She holds it close to her face, studying it like it's a map she wants to figure out. Minutes pass in silence. Everyone watches her carefully. I can't take it anymore; the only thing keeping me sane is staring at the calming hues of the stone.

I finally crack.

"Can I have my apple back?" I say, my voice gaining a crazy-person edge.

Woah, wait a moment. The word just slipped out of my mouth. Apple, stone, same difference. Chairs creak and everyone looks at me with expressions of concern.

Thomas cracks a teasing smile and says, "They are *so* very similar, Jack."

"They are not, Thomas, sir," Kappa interjects.

Give me a break, I'm hungry, I want to say.

Cole grabs the fruit and hands it to me carefully, as if I might try to eat his arm off. I exhale and bite into it. It's the most delicious thing ever, and no one can convince me otherwise. Cali watches me with a pouty face, and Thala notices.

"Okay, how about you six," she says, setting down the stone and pointing at my little squad with a huff of impatience, "go off to dinner while we talk about plans to liberate your camp."

We get up.

"The cafeteria is on Floor Two, assuming you know how to use the elevator," Thala adds.

I grab the stone off the table as we leave, just as a precaution. She looks up, but she doesn't seem surprised by my action. It morphs back into a snug-fitting bracelet. My mom glances at me and smiles. As the wall opens, I see her lean forward on the table, using her hands to explain something urgent to Thala. Starving, we trek off in the direction of the elevator.

"Jack, wait!"

It's Cole. We all turn to face him. He smiles at me, but his eyes drift down to my bracelet.

"Yes?" I answer impatiently, wanting to get food.

"May I share a word with you?" He glances at my friends. "In private, please?"

"Oh, no problem." I turn back to the group. "Can you guys wait at the elevator for me?"

They nod and walk away.

Cole leans against the closed wall, his smile gone. He stares me directly in the eye. His face really does look old—not physically, but emotionally, like he's experienced the full history of the world. Like he's an ancient soul trapped inside a child who has seen more than a lifetime of war.

"Tell me something, Jack," he says quietly. "What do you wish to accomplish with my stone?"

"*Your* stone?" I ask. "What do you mean?"

"I crafted it many years ago. You most likely do not know the stone's origin, being so young. Decades ago—maybe more than a century, when the first effects of Evil radiation started giving humans abilities—an element was found. It was the same element that contained the radiation that gave people abilities: the element Potestatemium."

"Wait, wait, wait," I say, holding up my hands. "Are you telling me that you were there all those years ago?"

"That is correct. I was only a child when the element reached humans. I was twelve—one of the few who survived the radiation," he murmurs bitterly. "Everyone else who survived or wasn't affected lived, grew old, and died. I had only aged a year, if not less than that. I lost family and friends, and I watched as generations rose and fell, including the last of my Good team. Throughout that time, I studied Potestatemium, and eventually I made the stone—a solid object of pure Potestatemium. I lived with it for a few years and observed its effects on me, and on other people, with and without abilities.

"I noticed the way it strengthened people with abilities, enhancing their power. It wasn't long before the teams learned of it. If they had gotten their hands on it, they might have used it to bring their enemies down, and the rest of the world with them. I hid the stone in a once-beautiful city, a place marked by so much radiation that it would be impossible to use machines to find it."

I stare at Cole in silence, taking in his past and imagining myself in his place. It'd be horrible to watch all my friends grow up without me, especially being just a child.

"Wow," I breathe. "That's amazing you did that, but what does any of this have to do with me?"

"I want to know if my creation is safe with you," he says simply.

Safe with me?

"But, *why* me?" I ask.

"Ah, yes, the big question," Cole says. "It seems to me that your ability is the most compatible with the stone, though I haven't known you long enough to figure out why. Some would say all of this is just a strange coincidence; others may say it is a blessing. But whichever way you see it, I want you to know you and the stone are interconnected now. The stone is sentient, and it will connect with your mind. No one can take it from you unless you want them to."

"That's pretty neat," I mutter. I flash back to when I was floating around and accessing Nora's memories. "Hey, Cole? I have a question."

"Go ahead."

"So, twice the stone took me out of my body, and I could see the auras of the people next to me. The usual color that I've seen is the same as the stone, but there was one person in particular whose light was red," I explain, trying my best to describe it.

Cole blinks and gazes at the ceiling, then back at me. "That is odd. The stone has never shown me an aura, but I believe it. And I'd expect the stone to identify Potestatemium similarly to itself. If it classifies someone as different … aha! The person you're talking about, perhaps the boy with purple eyes?"

"Yes, it's Travis."

"Oh, yes, that makes a lot of sense. It may be that he's affected by a different element or radiation altogether, which is why the stone identifies him differently. I'm not entirely sure, but I do hope this helps you."

"Yes it does, thanks," I say.

"Yes, of course. So, back to my previous question. What do you want to do with the stone—with this power?"

"I—I don't know," I answer honestly. "It's such a big responsibility, and I'm kind of scared. But at the same time, I want to do something. If I have the power to change the world, I want to use it for good. Not for the Goods, or any team, but for the people who need it. The people who are too weak, or afraid—I want to change things for them for the better."

I don't know where the words are coming from, but I mean each and every one of them.

"Thank you, Jack." Cole glances over his shoulder and rubs his head sheepishly. "You should probably go eat."

We shake hands again, and I turn to go.

"That took a while," Cali complains when I get to the elevator.

"Sorry." We step into the elevator and press the button for Floor Two.

* * *

The cafeteria is mostly empty, just a big space with a couple of tables out and an old man mopping the floor. It reminds me of the Dining Hall, except it has windows that let in golden rays. We're directed to an empty food line where we're allowed to get whatever we want. The food is fresh and warm, and the scents of baked bread, roast beef, and some sort of fruit juice intertwine and fill the air with a delicious-smelling aroma. I don't think I've ever inhaled my food so quickly.

Before we even make it to the door to go back to the meeting, a soldier, who insists he has orders from Thala, leads us through the clean halls to the elevator. I've only ridden the elevator a few times, but I'm really starting to hate it. We stop on a new floor, and the soldier guides us to a room with one bed, furry carpets on the floor, a separate bathroom, and a window. A few desks and chairs line the walls. It's a luxury I'm not used to.

This journey has been long—too long.

"When will we get to go home?" I mumble. "I'm so worried about the camp."

Thomas sits on a chair and shrugs, leaning back against the front of the desk. Kappa sits cross-legged at his feet, watching the rest of us.

"The Evils should be holding most of your people hostage, after finding out your brother didn't have what they were looking for," Travis says as he sprawls out on the carpet.

"If they get the information about you out of the people they need, like your brother," Travis continues, "then they should know that you'd come back *some*time. Besides, there would be no point burning down a place they're holding under siege."

109

"Right," I say. "So what happens to everyone at the camp? How come the Evils are only holding *most* of them hostage?"

"They may keep the majority of the group locked in a certain place, while others may be, unfortunately, killed as examples," Travis explains. "Though it's still too early for anything like that. Trust me."

I nod, though I wish he'd said this sooner. It's not exactly reassuring, but it's something, and I'm grateful that he at least tried to comfort me.

Nora suddenly gasps. "I've got it!" Her gray eyes are filled with excitement.

"Well, spit it out," Travis says with faked boredom.

"Jack can dream-travel," Nora announces. "The first night we met, I used a beacon to pull you off track. A beacon works like a magnet to people with abilities similar to Jack's. I'm sure the stone works in a similar way."

I nod slowly.

"Well, you can go to your brother's dream tonight," she exclaims.

It's a good thought. Unfortunately, it's already been shot down.

"I can't control where *I* go when I sleep," I sigh. "Besides, what if he isn't asleep?"

My contradiction brings frustration to Nora's eyes, but stubbornness quickly replaces it. She stares at the ceiling, probably thinking about a solution or alternative.

"Maybe it will work since you have the stone with you," Cali suggests, most likely referring to my floaty time.

I exhale and nod. I might as well try. Out the window, I see the sun is setting. Little drops of fire rain down. Thala must be continuing her work with the "Land of Fire."

I hop onto the bed, hoping nobody was planning to use it. The stone pulses against my own pulse. It's been so long since I've actually gotten to sleep in a real bed, and even though it was just a couple of days ago, it feels like an eternity. I close my eyes, curl into a ball, and soon drift away into a shadowy slumber.

Chapter XVIII

Dreams

It's so much different than before. Noises screech and sing and groan and fight around me. The currents are stronger: it's pandemonium. I'm no longer in control.

Voices spin around me, saying random things.

"You came back!"

"Armadillo? Armadillo."

"I'm kicking you over the edge."

"Yes, I beat level ninety-nine!"

"Where am I?"

The voices, noises, and images crash down on me. I don't know what they mean, or if they're real. Sometimes I recognize my friends, but none of it makes sense.

I just want it to stop. It needs to stop. *Just stop. Stop!*

And then it does.

Eerie silence is all that is left. My ears ring with the weight of it. It's like my wish has come true, and I stand in a blank white space—standing, not floating as I did before.

I can't see any people or colors. Everything is white. I look down at my hands; the hues have been drained from them, too. The stone isn't on my wrist.

A brilliant flash of aqua blinds me momentarily. I search for the stone. It's floating in front of me, drifting away, slightly out of my reach. I try to run toward it, but it feels like I'm knee-deep in mud, or quicksand, sloshing around uselessly. I hold my breath and lean forward with all my might, fingers outstretched, my entire being pushing toward the stone.

My fingers wrap around it and suddenly I'm back, levitating in the center of the room. I see myself on the bed, shining once again. This, I'm familiar with.

Only one aspect of the scene has changed: the currents pulling at me are now visible strings. I'm attached to all of them.

Then I remember why I'm here. Dreams. I need to reach Nico in a dream. Despite the distance between us.

Following the strings to the window, I drift over and peer outside. I'm certain that each of these strings is a person from my camp. It's weird, but I'm as sure of it as I am that I have two feet.

I study each string carefully, but it's like looking at each piece of hay in a bale. It's impossible to scrutinize each string without going insane. I brush my fingers over them instead. One particular string calls out to me. It's rough and familiar, and I grab that thread, making the world around me swirl all together. The walls and colors and lights come together in a tangled gust of wind.

It breezes past me, ruffling my hair and brushing past my clothes, bringing with it the scent of dewdrops on grass and soil. The wind slips past me like an invisible river, and I'm suddenly sitting on a patch of fluffy grass, overlooking a beautiful sunset. In the distance is the city, with its familiar crumbling walls and gray atmosphere. Everything mixes together so gorgeously that it seems unreal. The green of the grass and tiny yellow and pink flowers are all blanketed by an orange sunset. The city stands tall, gray, and proud just on the horizon.

I need one person right now. Nico. The string sits in my lap. I rub my fingers over it and close my eyes. I reach out the same way I do when opening telepathic conversations. I open my eyes.

A figure forms beside me, sitting cross-legged. It's not Nicholas. I straighten up to get a look at the person's face. The Captain. His rugged features are battered, his sandy-blond hair a mess. Bandages run across his arms and face. Curiosity pricks me.

"What's going on at camp?" I ask.

The Captain whips his head around to see me, startled by my presence. An expression of horror washes over his face. I feel guilty for failing and for abandoning everything important to me. The last time I saw him was when I screamed and ran. So that he wouldn't get the stone.

A wave of nausea crashes over me as I realize that the reason we aren't safe, living life normally, is because of the stone. Because of me. The Captain knows its power, and there is a good chance he was trying to help me. I fight the urge to break down then and there, thinking about how I've endangered the camp and my friends over a rock that I selfishly refused to give up.

I unfurl my fingers to stare at the stone, sitting innocently in my palm, unaware of all that it has caused. I don't have time to gaze at it and contemplate my life decisions because the Captain motions with his arm to the city.

"The Evils brought back Nicholas Barret two days ago, telling us that they'd kill him if we didn't tell them

114

where the stone was." His voice is soft and ragged, as if he's sick.

I gasp, my voice caught in my throat. I don't want to ask the question, for fear of its answer. Is the reason Nico can't appear because he's dead?

The Captain turns to me and continues. "They decided not to kill him after I told them he was your brother. Somehow they found out you were the one with the stone. They knew you by name. Once they figured out that Nicholas wasn't, in fact, you, but someone close to you, they decided to hold him hostage. They've been using our people to their advantage. I imagine Nicholas is up guiding people through the hallways."

Relief washes over me, flooding my insides and watering my dry, worried heart.

The Captain sighs. "They know you'll come back. They intend to burn the camp down after they've gotten you, but maybe they'll spare us. You will come back anyway, yes?"

I nod. Of course I'm coming back. I don't care if it's dangerous, I'll never leave my camp behind like that again. The Captain nods as well and slumps his shoulders. He looks exhausted. I'm sure he's been trying his best to hold everything together, despite being in charge of only a small portion of my community.

"I have a question," I say.

The Captain raises his eyebrows.

"How did you know what the stone was, back at camp?"

The Captain sighs and fixes his dark eyes on the sky. "I was told stories of it by my captains and elders. It's not really new; the legend of the ability enhancer has been around for a while."

I think back to Cole's story of how he made the stone a long time ago. I guess it makes sense for the Captain to know of it if the teams do.

"But how did you know what it was without seeing it?" I question, still a bit confused.

"My ability." The Captain smiles. "You may not have known, but my ability allowed me to sense the stone. It was just a hunch, but I figured you found some form of ability-related technology. Whether it truly was the stone didn't matter, since it's my job to confiscate anything similar anyway."

We sit in silence for a few minutes. I've known the Captain my entire life, but for some reason it never occurred to me that he had an ability, or a real name, for that matter.

"I'll try to reach Nicholas for you when I wake," the Captain says suddenly. "Anything you'd like to tell him?"

I think for a moment. I close my eyes and say, "Tell Nico I'm sorry for what happened. Tell him to stay strong. Tell him that I found our parents, and that we're all okay. We'll be back soon, and we have help. But make sure not to tell the Evils."

I pause, then add, "Tell him that I miss him and that I love him. We'll be back, I promise."

I open my eyes.

The Captain nods and places his large hand on my head. He smiles and says, "I understand why you took the stone. No hard feelings, Barret. I'm proud of you …"

His voice starts to diminish, melting into a windy whisper. Around us, the world crumbles, first shattering like glass, then turning to dust and blowing away. The Captain is already gone. All that's left is the spot of grass I'm sitting on, and that is already tumbling away.

I'm falling.

As I fall into the void, I see Travis falling next to me.

"I'm trapped … time … died … don't forget the promise," he says, his voice fading in and out.

I yell at him, asking what he means. But he, too, fades away. I expect to see all my friends come tell me weird stuff as I fall, but no one appears. I just keep falling.

I crash onto the bed, sinking into my pillow, and I open my eyes. The room is dim. The window lets in a few dying beams of moonlight. My internal clock tells me it's early morning, but I'm not entirely certain.

Above me, a figure is perched on the edge of the bed, watching me wake up. Instinctively, I stretch my arms out and elbow the figure in the nose in self-defense.

"Ow, Jack!" a voice complains.

Thomas. I relax against the giant, cushy pillow. Thomas turns on a lantern, and his face comes into view. I sit up slowly and look around the room. We're alone. Just Thomas and me.

"Where's everyone else?" I ask.

Thomas smooths back his bangs, which flop promptly back over his forehead. "They're in a meeting with Ms. Thala. I decided to stay so that when you woke up, you wouldn't be confused. We can head to the cafeteria for breakfast after you get ready."

I nod in gratitude, hoist myself out of bed, and stumble to the bathroom, closing the door behind me. My shoulder is bruised but it doesn't hurt much, and my leg is doing better. The medicine must have worked.

Thomas and I make our way to breakfast, tracing our steps back to the cafeteria. We eat as much as we can. On our way out, we ask a tall rugged-looking man for directions to the meeting.

Once we're in the elevator, I tell Thomas about what happened in my dream.

He listens quietly for a moment before answering. "We need to get back, then."

"Right," I say.

The doors open, and we walk swiftly to the meeting, which is in the same room as yesterday. Thomas places a hand on the wall and the bricks fold away, revealing Thala and the others.

Chapter XIX

Preparation

Thala greets us. She's sitting at the far side of a round table with Nora, Travis, Cali, Kappa, my parents, and Cole. She fills us in on what they already discussed: today before sundown, we attack. The Evils apparently won't expect us at that time because that's usually when Goods perform their activities. Plus, they already wiped out all of the Good teams in the area. As far as I know, that's all Evils ever do—attack Goods and Indifferents.

"Of course, it's not a foolproof plan, but it's our best shot," Thala explains. "We cannot afford to lose this chance of saving the camp and the stone. If Cole is right about the stone, it plays a huge role in the fate of the world. The Evils could use it to wipe out the Goods and anyone who stands in their way, leaving the rest of the neutral world vulnerable. They would use it to manufacture more stones and give their soldiers abilities without the risk of death. The Evils outnumber every other side. With the stone, world domination would be easy."

I nod along, rubbing the stone with my thumb over and over, impatient to share my dream.

"Which is why I think we should leave it here," Thala says.

I sit forward. "No, I'm taking it."

"We can't risk it being captured."

"It can't be taken from him," Cole pipes up. "They're interconnected. Trust me, Thala."

"With all due respect, Cole, he's a *child*, and the thought of him coming with us is absurd, especially if he's bringing the stone," Thala argues.

Folding my arms, I stare at Thala and say, "This is *my* camp. In my dream, the Captain told me he—"

"Your friends told me you were going to meet *Nicholas* in your dream," my mom interrupts.

"He wasn't asleep. But he's fine, Mom. He's still doing his job," I assure her. "I traveled into the Captain's dream last night. He told me the Evils are keeping him alive so they can navigate the camp. The Captain also told me the Evils are planning to burn down the camp if I don't go back. I need to go back, and I need to find Nico."

"And if you get captured and killed?" Thala demands.

"It's dangerous, Jack," my dad says. "Thala's right, if you go back, you *could* get injured or worse."

Nora smacks her palm on the table. "We won't let that happen."

"That's right," Travis adds. "We're taking him with us."

"Right," Thomas repeats. "We need him."

Cali smiles at me, places a hand on my shoulder, and echoes, "Right."

"Left," Kappa inputs. "I will also protect Thomas sir's friend."

Cole glances at me. "I believe in Jack. He may be inexperienced, but he has a strong spirit and good friends who will defend him."

A warm sensation rises in my chest, making me grateful to my friends for standing up for me. Here, I'm important to them. I'm needed.

Thala eyes me warily, then sighs and nods. "Okay, fine."

Travis sits forward, staring intently at me, and says, "Now, a little insight into the Evil team back at your camp. They expect you to come back, right? What they don't expect is for you to bring the Indifferents. Regardless, they are prepared for anything."

I sigh. He was part of the Evil team that captured my camp—I can only guess that he's correct. I've gotten accustomed to his presence, despite having a little bit of knowledge about what he's done and can do. But he's been through a lot. I believe in second chances, and he hasn't done anything to hurt our plans. Overall, he confuses me.

Cole looks up from the pile of papers on the table. "They may try to stop us, but if anything, we will only be slightly delayed. There are close to two thousand of us here. We are all capable of fighting, and we all have abilities. The Evil team does not stand a chance."

Travis nods. "We should outnumber the Evils. We have a good chance."

We all murmur in agreement. The Indifferents *are* powerful.

Thala adds, "Just because we live in the neutral zone most of the time, not bothering with what is happening in the world around us, doesn't mean that we are unable to defend ourselves and others who share our ideals. Perhaps after this, your camp will be interested in joining our ranks. It would benefit both of us. We can protect your camp, and you'll have a stable lifestyle."

I glance at Thomas, Cali, and my parents.

Shrugging, I answer, "I don't speak for my camp, sorry. My parents can tell the leaders about everything the Indifferents do, though."

Thala raises her eyebrows but nods, understanding what I mean.

"Now," she begins, "about the distance ..."

Thala and the others discuss the issues and solutions over traveling back to the city, going over the time and transportation.

Soon the meeting is over, and Thala sends us and a few escorts to a training room to prepare for the upcoming attack. She wants us to be able to defend ourselves efficiently.

The room is spacious, with large tinted windows that cast rays of light onto the back of the weapon rack to the right. There are a couple of stalls with doors to the left for changing and taking quick showers. The training room has mats on the tile floors and equipment hanging on the walls.

Our instructor welcomes us with enough friendliness, introducing herself as Adelyn. She's a tall woman with copper skin and thick braids, in her mid-twenties.

While I grab the training equipment—armor pads, batons, and helmets—as instructed, I hear her mutter, "Indifferents never had to fight another person's war. There is a reason we are called to be *indifferent*."

I toss training batons to everyone except Kappa, who explains she was programmed with battle techniques; her training is hardwired into her brain. Thomas fumbles when catching his baton, and Cali misses hers completely. She sheepishly retrieves it off the ground. Nora and Travis catch theirs easily, making me feel bad for Thomas and Cali. I should have thrown their sticks better.

Adelyn grabs her own baton and demonstrates different techniques with it. She shows us how to effectively get out of someone's grip by twisting their arm and putting them in a choke hold. She explains how to disarm someone who has a weapon, by kicking or knocking it out of their hand, twisting their pinky finger, or ducking and elbowing them. We're taught the weakest points on the body, such as the eyes, throat, shins, and the tops of the feet. I try to learn each one as best as I can, but this whole fighting stuff is new to me. I mean, I only tackled a lady and got thrown into a wall once.

We practice against dummies, and Adelyn intently observes the way we carry out the moves. When she figures out our strengths, she works with us individually to help improve and build our "styles."

Thomas, Cali, and I are all in the same boat. Everything is hard at first, but we each find what works. Nora does pretty well, adapting to each technique with a bit of spice, changing up one routine with a few extra swings or kicks.

When I ask her about her training, she says, "Admittedly, I've gotten a bit rusty, but I'm starting to get back in the flow of it."

I look over my shoulder to see how Travis is doing. He's flawless. He copies each movement Adelyn shows him. You'd think he already knows them by heart.

Adelyn pauses and asks him if he's trained with someone using these techniques before.

"No, none of the Evil teams ever got personal trainers," he says. "The one thing we were taught was to imitate and study all motions so that we could use them against opponents we've only recently met. Then we wouldn't need to learn anything else."

"There's always room for improvement," Adelyn says before flipping him over her shoulder and standing with one foot on his chest.

Quick as a flash, he grabs her leg and trips her. He gets up and stands over her. Smirking, he says, "Sure."

As we continue to practice, I start to have trouble focusing. Thinking about ambushing our camp and liberating it stirs up a nervousness in me that makes my heart thump and my fingers tremble.

What if something goes wrong? What if we can't beat them?

After mulling over this thought for a while, Travis tells me to shut up, meaning that I've been broadcasting. You'd think he'd be used to it by now. He tells me to shut up again.

The shadows cast by the weapons rack have moved, indicating that time has passed, and I'm getting hungry again. Adelyn directs us to get with a partner and spar, to practice with another person rather than a dummy. I pair up with Thomas, Cali goes with Nora, and Travis challenges

124

Adelyn. Kappa sits in the corner, watching us intently and occasionally shouting encouragement to Thomas.

Thomas has strings tied around his baton. While in combat, Thomas's technique is to throw his baton around the side of my head, purposely missing so the strings loop around my neck. He grabs the baton, pulls me in with the strings, and smacks me lightly. The first few times he does it, I'm surprised, but I soon learn to duck and kick him in the shins.

Adelyn tells us to prepare for the journey by picking out weapons and more protective clothing. We'll be heading out soon, she promises.

Anxiety pricks me like static shocks as I decide on my new change of clothes, wondering again if we'll be able to do it, wondering if life will ever be the same again.

But do you want it to? a voice asks.

I can't answer. I don't know. Over the past couple of days so much has changed, yet I'm not sure if it was all necessarily bad. I created a close bond with five friends, and I found my parents and a super-camp. But I let my brother go, and I'm not sure if either of us will survive this upcoming battle and see each other again. I exhale and sift through the clothes, trying to find something my size and style, though I'm not too picky.

I choose a dark grayish-green coat over a plain gray shirt, and long black pants with my usual boots. Being the first one changed, I walk over to the weapon rack and look outside. The sun is a bit lower in the sky than before, and a group of Indifferents stand near the building.

In the weapon rack are knives, guns, sticks, bombs, and more types of blades than I've ever seen before. I handle the ones that catch my eye, but they don't feel right. All the weapons appear either too harsh or too hard to use. Weird, but it's like the dart gun. If I can't shoot a needle that puts people to sleep, how can I shoot someone with the intent to put them to sleep for good? But I know I have to fight. Back then, I was scared. Now, I'm scared and prepared. I'm ready for this battle, and I'd do anything for my camp, and to make this world a better place.

The stone shakes on my wrist and moves toward my hand. With a sudden blue flash, I'm holding a familiar aqua dagger. The stone. It morphs from a dagger into a gun, into a baton, and back into a bracelet on my wrist. Throughout the entire transformation, it doesn't drop out of my hand. Cole was right. It's stuck with me for good.

I smile. Though I'd never go out of my way to hurt anybody with a knife or a gun, knowing the stone will become whatever I need it to be means that it'll do nicely.

I stare out the window and realize how much I miss wandering the city by myself, contemplating life, and helping out my camp. I know nothing will be the same again, and that's okay, but the change is still scary, and the stakes are high. During these past few days, I've come to terms with everything that's happened to me—becoming important and being able to change the world. It's terrifying, and I feel like I'm being forced to grow up too soon, but this is my chance to impact something. Plus, the thought of going back and finding my brother makes me determined.

Travis appears wearing a black coat, a new purple scarf that rises to his chin, and long pants like mine. His eyes flick over my choice of weapon, and he nods approvingly. He grabs several knives, a gun, and a pack of bullets, and straps them to his belt.

Nora shows up in a simple white shirt with a gray coat tied at her waist. On her hands are fingerless gloves, compliments of Cole: they're the same style and color as his, which is cute.

Soon after, Thomas comes in and then Cali. Thomas is wearing a bluish-gray outfit similar to mine, while Cali has a yellow one like Nora's, minus the gloves.

Nora immediately picks a thin sword that shimmers, similar to the one from her memory. Thomas grabs a lasso with bristles on the end. Cali takes knives. She slips them into little sheaths on her back.

Adelyn smiles at us, but there is worry in her eyes, and I recall her comment from earlier.

Indifferents never had to fight another person's war. There is a reason we are called to be indifferent.

"You are all very strong," she says, "and I hope we all live to see each other again."

We all thank her, and she hugs each of us, Kappa too. We go down to the cafeteria, Adelyn's last instruction being dinner. Thala meets us after we finish eating, and we follow her outside for the long journey back.

A large gathering of people stand waiting beside the building. There are majestic beasts, which I've only ever heard of, called horses. The horses are a multitude of colors: brown, red, white, black, and a mix. Their necks dip to the ground, allowing them to eat the dried, half-alive grass, and their flowing manes and tails swish in the cool breeze. Some kick the air with their muscular legs, while others calmly wait with an air of quiet patience.

Thala turns to address the crowd, clapping a few times to get their attention.

"We will park the horses just outside the city limits and go on through the city from there. If we fall into trouble, some of the group will split to take care of it and catch up with us from behind." The experience in her voice makes me wonder how many times she has stormed cities.

Thala leads us to the front line where the horses wait.

"We haven't ridden horses before," I inform her, motioning to Thomas and Cali.

"Don't worry. You'll be riding with someone since we don't have enough rides for each person."

That makes sense.

A young man with a short ponytail holds his rough hand out to me at Thala's command, and I climb onto the cream-colored animal with his help. We sit on a long, padded seat—a saddle—molded for our comfort.

Soon we are all mounted. The sun isn't as high in the sky as before, but it'll be a while until it starts to set. We're hours away from the city; the journey on Kappa took us all morning, and she was running pretty quickly. The horses are fast, though, so it should take around the same time.

Thala whistles, sharp and clear, riding out in front of us on a beautiful black stallion whose coat gleams in the sunlight.

We ride in sets of three, forming a long, yet orderly line. As we start to gallop faster, I'm forced to strengthen my hold on the man in front of me so I don't fall onto the rocky path. Being too heavy to ride a horse, Kappa runs beside the group, keeping up effortlessly.

My stomach churns with apprehension when I think about my last encounter with the Evils. We didn't fight them directly because we were busy running away, and for good reason, but I still hear their cruel voices ringing in my ears, shouting for the stone.

I try to zone out for the rest of the ride, after finding that my emotions not only affect humans, but horses as well.

Soon the city is in view, a familiar figure in this confusing and chaotic world. The broken buildings and permanent fog welcome us grimly, foreshadowing the mood of the battle ahead. The shapes of the buildings get bigger and bigger.

We pass the path where my friends and I escaped and circle around the perimeter of the city, stopping at a large tunnel that looks suspiciously like a sewer drain. It dips into a large muddy trench that could once have been a river.

Remembering the pipe room, the place I almost drowned, sends shivers down my back. But the stone throbs gently against my pulse, as if reminding me that that was where I found it.

We dismount and stretch our legs. Mine are sore, despite the fact that I've been sitting the entire time.

The riders guide their horses to portable posts they've drilled into the ground. Thala yells orders over the ranks, reassuring them that though the journey was sudden and hasty, they shouldn't be nervous.

"Our society is growing as more Indifferents join us. We fight for them just as we'd fight for ourselves, knowing that they are building the community. As we get closer to expanding the neutral zone and finding peace among our citizens, we push for the future and for these people. We are the last, we are the remainder. We are indifferent to this war of Good and Evil, holding out until it ends. But when the war messes with our fellow men, women, and children, what will we do? Will we help these people trying to hold out as well? Will we fight for our beliefs and theirs? Will we add to our ranks? Are you with me?"

The army cheers. She raises her fist and pumps it once in the air before putting it over her heart. The troops all raise their hands and salute back with the same motion. It seems to renew their energy.

We plunge into the tunnel. Back into the darkness I go.

Chapter XX

Coming Home

Okay, I'm not going to lie. I'm nervous. As we march through the dark tunnel, my heart is racing faster than the horses did. Thala says we're going in "blind," in case there's anyone at the end of the tunnel. We don't want anyone to see us coming.

Thomas and Cali huddle shoulder to shoulder with me. Kappa walks behind Thomas, her eyes closed so as not to light up the tunnel. We walk up front behind Travis, Nora, Thala, and a couple of adults. My parents were needed back at the Indifferents building to round up the rest of the Scouts still in the area and prepare for the journey back.

I make out the hushed whispers of Travis, Nora, and Thala a few feet ahead, quietly discussing the route to the camp.

Proving Thala's point about going in blind, three unsuspecting enemies stand outside the opening. Thala rushes at them and takes them by surprise, quickly bringing all three of them down single-handedly. She flips the first one over so hard, it knocks him out. Then she throws his body at the second two, and they sprawl into the wall. The rest of us emerge into the foggy unknown.

I'm blinded temporarily by the light of day, but my eyes soon adjust. We head into the destroyed city quietly. I gaze up at the familiar gray steel and concrete structures. The only noise comes from the soft crunching of our boots in the gravel. Nora and Travis work with Thala to guide us back to camp based on direction. I've never been this way before, so I can't really help. The street is too open, and the few landmarks I recognize are ones I always tried to avoid.

I know we're supposed to be silent, but I can't take it anymore. "It's so quiet," I whisper to Thomas, not bothering with MindSpeak. It's too quiet. And that bothers me. The Evils are waiting for me, and that alone is intimidating, but the most unnerving thing about this whole ordeal is the silence. The squawking birds have vanished. The wind has abandoned the broken buildings, and the creaks and groans from shifting boards that used to make up the unsteady beat of the city are gone. It feels ... empty.

"Yeah, it's weird. It wasn't like this when we left," Thomas leans in and mutters back.

Cali looks over and nods. "You know where we are?"

"Kind of."

It feels unfamiliar without the usual noise.

We walk past a weathered statue of an angel and under a couple of bridges before stumbling into a dead end.

Nora, Travis, Thala, and a few Indifferents stare with puzzled expressions at the roadblock. We've marched into a U-shaped area, completely closed in by walls and buildings, with no alleys leading around.

Cali, Thomas, and Kappa stand next to me.

Thala turns to Nora and grumbles, "What now? I thought you knew the way."

"I already told you," Travis answers. "We knew the way from the path we took last time we were here. We've taken a different route now, so all we know is the direction the base is in."

"According to my compass, we're going in the right direction," Nora adds, pulling out a small circular device with letters and a little arrow in the middle.

The arrow spins for a second before pointing left.

The pattern in the rubble and the buildings looks familiar. I feel like I've been here before.

Thala sighs. "Then what do you suppose we do about this wall? We can't just smash through it. It's too high, and using a bomb would be too loud."

I study the wall, and realization hits me like a ton of bricks. I *know* this wall. I've been all over the city. I've never scaled this particular wall, but I recognize it from some of my other journeys while on top of the buildings.

"We climb!" I say triumphantly.

Thala turns to face me with an expression that tells me she thinks I'm insane.

I hop up and down, still excited, and place my hand on the wall, which is craggy and has little platforms and beams jutting out of it.

"When I scavenge stuff for the camp, I always travel up high, over the buildings. When I had to go on the ground, I used alleys. But traveling over the roofs of buildings is a lot faster and safer."

"Jack, that's a great idea!" Nora says, awestruck. "I can't believe I didn't think of that before. I mean, that's what we did when getting away from your camp."

133

My face flushes in embarrassment, and I shuffle over to the far end of the wall that connects to the building on the right.

"I'm going to find the best way up," I mumble to Thala.

She gives me a thumbs-up, smiling, and turns to address her army, telling them to sit tight for a while.

Travis walks up to me. "I'll come with you," he offers.

I shrug and nod, grateful for his company. A little thought drifts to the front of my mind, painting a warm picture, reminding me how much I've come to trust my little circle of friends over the past few days, despite our differences. Before, I wouldn't have gone anywhere with Travis, but he's proven a reliable and loyal friend. He's been through so much, losing his parents and his team, and yet he hasn't given up. Now, I'll gladly encourage his help with scaling a wall.

Travis looks at me as if he can read my mind, and unfortunately, he probably can. He only gives me a swift nod, but I'm sure he feels the same.

I scan the metal edges that stick out of the wall and notice a pattern. Some ledges are close together, some so close that they form steps. Some have big gaps in between them, and other ledges are just big enough to fit one foot on. I wonder if this used to be a staircase. Everything in the city was wrecked before we started living here.

I leap at the first few rungs. They're a bit high up, but I'm able to reach them and climb up to a small platform. I roll onto the ledge. Travis climbs up behind me a bit more gracefully.

Above me is a bar that sticks out like a pin. The next platform is a little far, but I decide to take a risk.

I hang from the rail above my head and rock back and forth. Once I have enough momentum, I swing forward and let go. A collective gasp sounds below me as I shoot off the bar and barely catch the edge of the platform with my toe. I windmill my arms and grasp a handhold a few inches above my head, so I'm standing up on the platform. Hugging the wall, I let out a shaky breath. I'm about twenty feet above the ground, and honestly, I don't think falling is such a good idea.

I wait a few minutes, cursing myself for risking that leap. There must be a safer way to go—one that doesn't involve me soaring to my death.

The next jump is impossible, so I need to think fast. It's well over my head, farther than my arms can reach. To go sideways I'll have to learn how to fly, and there are no grooves or edges I can use to climb vertically. At least, none safe enough to support my weight.

While I stand there wondering what to do, the stone flashes against my hand, and suddenly I'm holding my weapon. I'm not sure what to use it for. Thankfully, Travis does.

"Use the knife to climb!" he calls up to me. He motions stabbing the wall. I raise my eyebrows.

It's my only option, and it can't hurt to try.

I thrust my knife into a crack in the wall. It slices through the bricks like butter. I carve in a little handhold so the others will have something. Grabbing the knife with both hands, I use all of my upper-body strength to pull myself up.

As someone who's always climbing, you'd think this would be easy for me. But by the time my chest is level with the hilt of the blade, I want to drop down and give up.

I catch my breath and find another crack in the wall above my head. Carefully digging my fingers into the bricks, I slide off of the blade. Now I'm hanging by one arm. Fire jolts down my fingers into my joints and my chest. My hand is scraped and burning from having to scrabble at the bricks, but I persevere.

I look down to grab the blade and there's Travis, positioning himself to catch me. On the ground, my audience is staring up at me in horror.

I snatch the knife out of the wall and stab the bricks above my head.

One more time, I think.

I shift my hands to the hilt of the blade.

I dangle there, not wanting to do another pull-up. The world is cruel. But I find the strength to do it. As I stand up on top of the wall, I pull my knife out and it turns back into a bracelet. The wall is as wide as an average city sidewalk, connected to the building on the other side.

I'm pretty proud of myself for scaling a thirty- or forty-foot wall without dying.

I lean over the edge of the roof and give a thumbs-up to Thala. Travis makes it up the wall using the handholds I made and starts walking along it. He suddenly stops.

I reach out my hand. "Come on—"

But Travis's eyes are locked on something behind me. He draws his weapon and shouts a warning. I swivel around, only to be kicked in the chest and sent halfway over the edge.

I grip the ledge and search for my attacker, my mind blanking with panic. If I fall, that's it.

A tall, masculine figure dressed in black towers over me. Dread settles in my throat. The man crouches and holds a gun to my forehead. I gulp, knowing it's probably not loaded with darts.

"You're the Barret kid," he rumbles, glancing down at my glowing bracelet. "Hand it over—"

A dark shape flies over my head and barrels into the man. Travis stands over him, his ruffled hair windswept, the dagger in his hand pointed at the man's throat. The gun is several inches away from his boot.

"Travis, what are you doing?" the man splutters.

Travis replies smoothly with a shrug. "I'm kicking you over the edge."

He lands a hard blow to the man's side with his boot, promptly sending him over the side of the building. People on the ground shout. I wince as the man's cry ends abruptly with a harsh *crack*. Travis picks up the gun, loots the bullets, and holds out his hand to me.

I take it without question. "Y—you kicked ... You *murdered* him."

"No one threatens my friends. He was about to do the same thing to you. It wasn't my first kill anyway, and it won't be my last. We're going to battle, Jack."

"I—I know ... I'm just ... Don't do that again."

137

He pats my shoulder, his eyes betraying no regret for killing his former ally. Leaning over the edge, he repeats the thumbs-up I gave to Thala.

She barks something I can't hear, and the Indifferents surge up the wall, using their own weapons and the ruts I made with the stone. Kappa backs away a few feet, then sprints up the wall. She's one of the first on top.

Travis and I help as many people onto the ledge as we can. Kappa, under orders from Thomas, goes down and carries people up in seconds. Within the same time it took me to climb, half of the army is standing next to us on our ledge or on neighboring buildings, helping their comrades. Soon, everyone is up.

Nora, Cali, Thomas, and Kappa wade through the huge group to the front, joining Travis and me.

"Onward!" Thala commands.

I give the first example of leaping from building to building, crouching before I spring, spreading my feet apart, and occasionally grabbing my knees and rolling. The stone glows brighter, sensing my energy.

We move at a more urgent pace. Time for the ambush is running out. We pass from roof to roof fluidly, the entire group now running across buildings and jumping without hesitation.

With me in the lead, we soon make it to the camp, looking down at it from a nearby building. The ground level is heavily guarded, and keeping watch on the roof are a few unsuspecting sentries. They stand there as if nothing is wrong, as if they've had that job all their lives. It's only been two days, and they act like they own the place.

The Evils invaded, and they kidnapped my brother; the people of my camp are meaningless to them, and it makes me mad. Once unimportant and in the background, I now have the power to change everything and save my brother. Nico needs me, and more than anything, I have to not only be a good brother but also a good friend.

We crouch, eyeing the Evils and moving without making a noise.

Thala whispers to me, "I'm told you have the ability to broadcast thoughts to others. Can you repeat what I'm about to whisper to you to the army?"

"I can open a broadcasting chain that you can speak on, if you'd like," I suggest. "I'll begin it with a thought, and all you have to do is think what you're going to say."

"Doesn't sound too hard," she says.

I open a thread, projecting it at the army, then I signal to Thala to start: *"Go."*

At first, her thoughts are faint, but as she goes, the words get louder. *"We're going to hit them hard and from all angles. Our main goal is to drive them out of the city, so you don't need to kill them all at the site. Remember, we are not only fighting for Jack and his friends, but for the stone, for the innocent, and for our fellow Indifferents."*

The Indifferents are surprised by the MindSpeak at first, but they all focus on Thala as if she's speaking regularly.

Thala rests her eyes on me for a second before adding to the thread, *"And if you see Jack, make sure the Evils don't get the stone from him. It's more important than any of us realize."*

Nora picks up the message, saying, *"Make sure you only attack Evils! We don't want to hurt the prisoners inside the camp."*

Everyone nods, and I close the thread.

Thala unsheathes her sword and raises it up to the sky. "Indifferents, ATTACK!"

The army pounces on the camp like an animal, crouching, springing, and rolling to break the fall. They break off into groups and spread out to all the entry points, quickly dealing with each.

Unsure of where to go, I follow Nora, Cali, Thomas, Kappa, and Travis into battle. We slip into the same hatch that we escaped from yesterday morning.

Together, we storm the camp.

Chapter XXI

Unstoppable

Despite my lack of battle skills, I take the lead. There's a note on the ladder—a simple paperclip folded into the shape of a star, pointing to the door to our left. At the door is another one facing the left corridor. I smile. Nico.

The six of us march into the dark hallway and through the corridors. It feels so natural, being in the halls again, that I almost forget why we're here. Then we turn a corner, and I'm yanked back to reality. Face to face with the enemy.

Evils fill the hallway, six people across. They all wear black, some with hues of deep red or purple. They don't seem to be aware of the attack going on in the rest of the building. When we approach, they snap to attention, raising their weapons and scowling at us.

"What are you five doing outside your detaining rooms?" a woman with red hair demands.

I roll my shoulders. Can we take them?

Nora steps forward and replies, "What are you doing outside your home? You don't belong here."

The one who questioned us steps forward and frowns. "Hmm. Actually, I haven't seen any of you around—" Her eyes go wide. "Travis? What are you doing here? You've been marked a *traitor*!"

That's Travis's cue to step forward. He balls his hands into fists that are still wrapped in his old, ripped scarf. In the dim light, I can just make out the faded red and purple markings in his hair, and the scar, deeply embedded in his face, drawing out his pale features.

I study how he and Nora look together in the hallway and hope to see them like this more.

Nora's frizzy black hair is tied in her bandana, her cocoa skin washed yellow in the light of the lanterns. Her gray eyes capture the storm brewing overhead in the tense air.

"Natasha," Travis says, addressing the lead Evil, "you know exactly why I'm here."

Natasha snarls. She draws her knife and charges at Travis. I yank Nora back as Travis whips out his dagger and intercepts Natasha's blade.

Cali, behind me, whispers, "Should we help him?"

I don't answer. Our enemies are blocking the path, but they stand, entranced by the fight. Natasha's fiery hair flies around her face as she brutally pursues Travis. He doesn't back down, but she seems to be pushing him into a corner.

She's as good as him, if not better. I stand frozen once again, watching my friend fight another powerful lady.

Just as I decide I need to stop observing from the sidelines, a boy with rust-red hair appears from the tunnel behind the Evils. I grin at him, excited to see him again so soon.

"Jackie! You came back! I—"

An Evil in front of him turns around and backs him into the tunnel with his weapon to his chin and his hand over his mouth.

I let out a guttural cry and launch myself into the line of Evils. The stone transforms into a glowing knife, warming up against my hand. I try to remember the techniques I learned, but it seems I don't need to. I fight without thinking, letting my body act on autopilot. The Evils yell at me and I snarl in return. I'm locked in battle with one Evil, a tall boy around Travis's age with a wicked knife. In my hand, the stone elongates into a pipe, and I smack him in the head before he gets a chance to do anything.

I'm vaguely aware of Thomas, Cali, Kappa, and Nora drawing their carefully picked weapons and going to war. I want to keep an eye on my friends, but it's hard to do that and concentrate on not getting skewered at the same time. Besides, my main goal is Nico.

I turn around and connect blades with another Evil. Yet another attacks me on my right. I duck, pushing the first one away with my blade. I glance back to find Nico, but he's not there. My heart plummets, sinking with dread. I return my attention to the enemies in front of me.

Evil One swings his blade, and I deflect it. Evil Two tries to kick my legs out from under me, but I manage to sidestep. My vision is clear, and I'm calm. I notice everything going on—how Evil One keeps trying to preoccupy me, leaving Evil Two to attack while I'm distracted. Soon I'll miss something. I need to act now.

I step back and crouch as if to roll away from them. Instead, I pick up a rock with a star on it by the wall— another note from Nicholas. They tense up, prepared to catch me if I try to run. I pop up and lunge at Evil One. He swipes for me, but I turn and thrust my shoulder into his chest. He falls to the ground. Evil Two jumps for me, but I throw the rock at her.

She catches it reflexively, and I use the distraction to jump at her and knock her out with the hilt of my blade. I search for any sign of my brother, but he's gone. I clench my teeth in frustration. He must have fled, or that Evil took him.

Evil One stands back up and charges at me. I sidestep and push him into the wall. I don't want to kill anybody, but I want this fight finished so I can find my brother.

"You're real annoying," Evil One tells me, wiping his mouth.

"So are you," I say.

He takes offense at that and charges at me again, his knife aiming at my chest. The stone shocks me, giving me a cue. I duck and roll past his feet, then come back up and knock him in the head while he's still facing the other way. I stare at the stone, not realizing it was helping me until now. Pretty neat.

I see Thomas, Kappa, and Nora finish off three more Evils, while Cali takes on two more by herself. She seems to be taking care of herself just fine. Using MindLift, she makes one enemy fly and crash into the other.

I turn back to Travis and Natasha, hoping they both survived and called it a tie, making peace and leaving each other alone. Instead, Travis is standing over Natasha, who's unmoving.

I want to hope she's only unconscious. I don't always get what I want.

Travis faces us, his eyes dull and sad. This is more emotion than I've ever seen in him before. His shoulders slump and he's trembling slightly. His dagger is splattered and still dripping with blood.

"She was my friend," Travis sighs, his voice filled with grief. "I couldn't—I didn't want ..."

I walk up to him and whisper, "I know. I'm so sorry."

He blinks, takes in a shaky breath, and wipes his weapon on his coat.

"No time to cry now," he says, his voice quiet. "I chose to take this side. There's no turning back."

I watch his mental shields go back up, the sadness fading away from his indigo eyes, leaving them empty. He clenches his jaw and moves forward, lifting his chin and pushing past us to wait at the tunnel entrance.

There's no turning back.

"Did you see Nico?" I ask the rest of my friends.

"No, sorry," Thomas replies. "I was too busy fighting."

"Who is Nico?" Kappa asks me.

"My brother. He has red hair and green eyes. He was just here."

"I did not," Kappa says.

Cali and Nora shake their heads as well. I close my eyes for a couple of seconds, angry with myself for letting him go. He could be hurt. I look back at the group.

145

"Is everyone okay?" I ask.

Cali nods and Thomas says, "Just a few bruises and scratches."

Nora gathers us around. "Let's move."

We run down the tunnel, following the clues, glancing into each room for prisoners or Nico. I only want to see him. A paperclip is tied on one of the strings of light, telling us to take a right. The walls can't mask the noise or smell of the battle, with gunshots and the clanging of metal ringing, and the reek of sweat and blood hanging in the air like fog.

We slide around a corner, and there it is. The major battle.

The hallway opens up to the Dining Hall. Tables and benches are all pushed against the walls or broken and scattered.

On the floor are hundreds who are wounded or worse. The lights in the Hall are unusually harsh and bright. The room is big enough to fit the entirety of Thala's army, minus the horses, but space is still limited. All around, heroes and villains fight to the death. The Evils are easy to recognize in their dark attire, but they're all a blur, fighting with the agility and power of predators.

We plunge into the battle, with my friends taking out Evils and me guarding myself while looking for any sign of my brother. To the left of me, Thomas swings his barbed lasso around, entangling Evils and knocking them out by bashing them into their comrades. Kappa's hands have changed into spikes. She whirls them around like blades, bronze arcs of destruction.

To my right, Cali and Nora fight side by side, trying to get past the hordes. Some enemies flee, and the Indifferents take off after them.

Random objects fly around the room, and from time to time, enemy soldiers are knocked out by an invisible force that I know is Nora. For a split second, I start to believe we're winning, but a stampede of Evils enters from one of the corridors and the battle is renewed.

About a third of our army is out of the Hall. Those in here are outnumbered.

I spot Thala fighting her way to an injured soldier. Time passes, each second in slow motion but still racing at the speed of light. With each opponent that comes at me, I feel my arms getting weaker, my legs refusing to stand. I want to collapse and hand over the stone. That's what we're fighting about, right? But I can't give up, especially with my brother somewhere in the camp. I inhale and duck just as a sword swings over my head.

I hear a rough voice shout, "Get it! The kid is here. Kill him!"

A sudden wave of déjà vu overcomes me at the voice. Suddenly, a dozen Evils turn in my direction, and I nearly choke.

Thala's voice erupts nearby. "Don't let them take it!"

The battle continues to rage, but now more Indifferents are making walls around me, watching my back, and attacking anyone who comes near. I feel honored, but part of me wonders how many of them are actually fighting for me or simply following orders.

147

Guilt stabs me as I realize how many innocents have given their lives for me. And the stupid stone.

"Jackie!"

I whip around to see Nico in the doorway of the corridor we came in from. I freeze. He smiles and starts to run toward me.

"Stay there!" I scream at him, not wanting to endanger him anymore.

Swimming through the sea of opponents, I chase back as many as possible, clearing a path through those near Nico, burning my way toward him. I'm halfway across the Hall, stepping over people who have fallen, but I'm still right in the middle of the battle. I keep my eyes forward, on my enemies and my brother. I don't want to see the fallen on the floor, the people sacrificed for the sake of the stone. Looking at them reminds me of how terrible this reality is, how people have to suffer because the wrong people are the ones making changes. It reminds me of how doubtful of myself I am, and how I always stand in the background, unsure of what to do.

You want to make a change, right? Why wait around? Are you scared?

No. I'm done. I'm finally done with being uncertain. I'm going to fight, even if it takes all that I have. I'm going to fight for Nico, for my camp, and for the whole war. I may be an Indifferent, but I won't stand in the background anymore. I push my way through the battle, fighting and taking down whomever gets in my way, even the Indifferents. I no longer care. The voice in my head focuses into a piercing scream, a battle cry that rips into the air and the minds of those around me. Evils and

Indifferents alike drop to the ground, and the ones able to move scatter, running out of the Hall.

I emanate panic and pain, though I feel strangely calm. I run toward Nico, using the distraction I caused to get through the Hall easily and unopposed.

Just as I get a couple of feet from him, he lurches to the side, hit by an invisible force. He cups his hand to his shoulder. There's blood. Lots of it. I inhale a sharp breath of panic and gently grab him and pull him to the side. I cradle him with one arm and smooth back his hair.

His eyes are dull, and he doesn't cry. He looks confused, maybe from the shock of being shot by a bullet that I'm certain was meant for me.

He blinks and murmurs, "You're here."

"Of course I am," I whisper.

"Is it bad?" he croaks.

I shake my head, not knowing what to say. Thomas sprints over to us and kneels beside me. His eyes widen at my brother's wound.

"What happened to him?" he yells.

I don't answer. My words are caught in my throat.

Thomas calls out for Kappa and she sprints over, knocking enemies out of her way. Cali arrives and says something to Nico, though he's passed out.

I glance up, looking around, though I'm not sure what I'm searching for. Behind us, Thala helps Kappa fend off a few Evils. Kappa is a war machine; she's probably the main reason so many Evils are out of commission.

Only around a hundred people remain in the Hall, still fighting. I spot Travis and Nora. Travis seems to have abandoned his dagger and now has a gun. He shoots down a few people, then looks back at me. Nora still has her glimmering sword, but her movements are slow and fatigued. I want to get up and help her, but I have to stay by Nicholas. I'm immobilized with uncertainty, unsure of what to do and say. Travis rips his gaze away and tackles someone charging at us.

Cali says something like, "Another one? Darn it," and runs off. Thomas pats Nico's head, tells him everything will be okay, and runs after Cali.

The noise fades out. I stare at my brother, his shoulder glistening crimson. Conscious again, he winces.

They did this. The Evils did this. Now my friends are fighting to the death, strangers I only met a day ago are battling it out for my camp, my brother is wounded, and I don't know how bad it is. My head pulses as I get up. Lightheaded, I stand in front of Nico and guard him. Occasionally, an Evil or two will come up to us, but they appear tired and their actions are slow. Either I take them down, or Kappa does.

Some of the Evils are crying or holding their heads in pain. I realize that I'm still broadcasting against only them. A rush of excitement flows through me at the thought of gaining more control of my ability, and even doing new things with it.

I continue broadcasting to the Evils and watching the battle. Scanning the Hall, I notice Travis has stopped fighting. He's staring at something near one of the entrances.

A boy appears. He walks calmly into the Hall, his aura radiating a sense of chaotic coolness. His dark outfit marks him as an Evil, but he doesn't seem fazed by my broadcast. His auburn hair shines in the harsh light, which washes over his tan skin, illuminating him and making him look like a ghost. He's focused on Travis like an owl hunting its prey.

A giant gun materializes in his hand.

Hefting his huge firearm up to his shoulder, he shouts, "Travis, you traitor!" He says it like it's the new motto of the Evil team, like it's something he's required to say. But his voice hides a thin layer of pain and contempt.

Travis is frozen, staring at the newcomer in horror.

Though the guy with the big gun looks like bad news, I don't want to go too far from Nico.

"Rowan," Travis chokes out, lowering his gun.

There's hesitation on his face, something I haven't seen in a while.

The auburn-haired dude, Rowan, growls, "Travis, how could you? Trade us for them? Seriously? Why?"

I find it a little unfair that Rowan would bombard him with so many questions, but he replies anyway.

"Rowan, I don't mean to hurt you. But what Evils do, what I've done before, it's wrong. This is wrong."

"You killed Natasha."

"I'm sorry … I'm so sorry."

Rowan bares his teeth, his bright amber eyes glittering. "I'm sorry too."

He lifts his gun, aiming at something near Travis. Nora. Travis gasps as Rowan pulls the trigger.

I cry out her name.

Boom.

Nora whirls around just as a bullet is fired. Travis runs to her from behind, passes through her like a ghost, and intercepts the projectile. Rowan blinks as if processing what happened. Nora shrieks. Cali and Thomas turn, their shoulders rigid with shock. All four of us, Rowan, Cali, Thomas, and me, surge forward and rush to Travis's side. Kappa notices Thomas running and walks through the crowd to see what the matter is. She stands over us, defending us while we grab Travis.

The battle seems to disappear. Cali and Thomas help pull him to the side where Nico is. Nora cups Travis's head in her hands. Her breath catches as he coughs, wincing. His coat is stained with blood.

Thomas follows my sightline to Rowan, standing motionless behind us, and turns to glare at him. Rowan dashes away, out of the Dining Hall, not looking back.

A flood of people washes into the Hall, armed with pieces of broken furniture. They yell, shouting names that echo through the Hall, a spoken memorial that fills the air. Then it dawns on me that these are my people. They drive the remaining Evils away, following them out. The battle is finished. All that remain are the dead, the wounded, and those trying to help them. Kappa kneels beside Travis now that the battle is over, her face expressionless, not fully understanding what just happened. She studies our faces, then looks at Travis and frowns, copying our emotions.

"Well ... we won," Travis mutters amidst the sound of groaning and crying from the other fallen.

I lean close to him and whisper, "Travis, please, hold on."

He smiles and shakes his head sadly. "It's okay, Jack. That ... That gun ... There's no going back."

"No! Not now!" Nora cries, hugging him.

Travis coughs again, his breath ragged, the light in his eyes fading. "It's not the end. Remember, you told me anything is possible. It's not the end ..."

His voice trails away, and his body goes limp. A scream erupts. Cali and Thomas sob, and Nora pounds the floor with her fist. Kappa puts her arm around Thomas in a gesture of comfort, but she tilts her head, unsure of why we're all so sad.

I finally turn away from Travis and the others and wipe my face on my sleeve. A medic has already gotten to Nico, who hugs me with his good arm. He's pale, but he doesn't look too pained.

"How are you feeling?" I ask him, a little surprised by the calm in my voice.

"Good," he replies quietly. "I'm so happy you're here."

"Me too. I was worried about you. The Captain explained a little bit about your situation, but what really happened?"

"I was taken back to camp by those Evils. They had everyone who lives in this building in the Dining Hall. Everyone looked scared. I saw that they killed Billy ..."

I recall the names being shouted during the last few minutes of the battle.

"They didn't hurt you while I was gone, did they?" I ask.

"No. The Captain stood up for me. But the Evils wouldn't let me go to sleep. They said they needed me to show them where everything was."

"You can sleep all you want after this," I assure him.

He smiles.

"I need to help out," I tell Nico. "You should sit down or something. I'll bring you some water."

"Okay, Jackie," he says.

After I get Nico's water, I join Cali, Kappa, and Thomas, and we help clean up. I aid the other wounded, including the Evils, bandaging wounds and passing around medicine and water from the kitchen. All I want is to keep myself busy, to try and forget everything.

Hours later, my arms aching from carrying buckets of water and bandaging the wounded, I see Nora get up. She suggests we take Travis outside to wait for the sunrise, so he can see the sun for the last time. A depressing thought, but I don't disagree, for Nora's sake. We pick up our fallen friend's body, and Nico leads us out. My vision blinks in and out as we carry him, and I feel lightheaded and dizzy from broadcasting so much, as if I might fall over or crash into a wall. But Travis is pretty light for a guy who seems so burdened all the time. When we get to the ladder, Kappa drapes him over her shoulder and carries him up.

We lay Travis's broken body outside on the roof. I gasp at the faded orange and purple of the sunrise, not realizing the war lasted through the night.

We each take turns saying something private to Travis. When my turn comes, I kneel next to him.

With a shaky voice, I whisper, "You are a hero. You'll always be a hero, no matter what you've done in the past. Thank you, Travis, for choosing the right path."

I hold my hand out, and my bracelet morphs back into an aqua stone. Sniffling, I grab Travis's dagger and cut the stone in two. I take his hand and put one half of the stone beneath his fingers. I know it's risky leaving such a powerful item unguarded, but I want him to have a part of the object he died to protect. And maybe, somewhere deep inside me, I want and hope with everything I have for it to save him. The stone glows warmly as it changes color. Scarlet turns to blue and then to a light shade of indigo as I let it go.

I lower my head and get up. Nora is the last to say goodbye. I can't hear what she says, but she puts a charm in his other hand. We all turn as one and head back to the hatch.

"Where should we bury him?" I ask. The half of the stone in my hand shakes and pulses against my skin.

It shines brighter than it has before. Confused, I glance back at Travis. Except, he's not there. I nudge Nora and she turns around. We all do.

"Captain Knight is gone," Kappa states.

The stone shakes violently in my palm again. I look down at it in surprise, and a bubble of hope forms in my mind. The stone's aqua color turns a shade of indigo before changing back to aqua.

Two words suddenly form in my mind. Travis's voice, much younger, back with kid-Nora playing that ball-word game.

Indigo. Faded.

I gaze up at the dawn and remember. Whatever happens, it's not the end.

Epilogue

For Our Future

It's been two months since the battle. Two months since Thala split her group, leaving some Indifferents here and taking the rest back to their main base. Two months since I watched as Thala rounded up her group on horseback, and they shouted their goodbyes and rode off into the dull sunset.

Both sides lost a great number of people. The Evils left the city, leaving behind their wounded and dead. Some of the wounded Evils pulled through, and we let them choose to leave or make new lives at camp. My parents came home and reported back everything they learned from their missions to the camp leaders. They also took some time off to spend with Nico. Cali and Thomas have stayed close to me for the most part, and now we work together, inseparable since the battle, except when they're called for a specific job. Kappa sticks around Thomas, helping to rebuild and move items.

Soft footsteps sound on the roof near the hatch behind me.

"Hey," Nora says.

I turn and smile at her. "Hey."

A lot has changed at the camp. Not only because we're now Indifferents, but also because we fought a war against Evils and won. We discovered that there is so much more to the world than our little city.

"What are you thinking about, Jack?" Nora asks, focusing her gray eyes on me.

For a second, I forget that I gained control over my broadcasting. Throughout the weeks, I've become more experienced with my ability, and now I no longer broadcast without willing myself to do so.

I shrug. Nora pats my shoulder and heads toward the hatch. I turn my eyes back to the horizon.

"Hey, Nora?" I say, twisting the glowing bracelet on my wrist.

She looks back. "Yes, Jack?"

"Do you think there are more like him?"

"What do you mean?"

"Travis. He joined the Evils, but in the end, he sided for a better cause. For peace," I say.

She blinks slowly, her gray gaze unreadable. "I'm not sure. What do you think?"

"I think that not every Evil is evil. Even if they don't know it. Some people may not be born with abilities, but we all have the ability to make a change."

Nora smiles and whispers, "I think so, too."

I face the sun again. Nora's footsteps recede, and I stare at what's left of the stone on my wrist. I have a lot of tasks ahead of me.

But for now, life is good. And though there are so many changes, I'm going to embrace them. This is the world I'm living in—a scary, exciting, broken, and beautiful place. But it's my present. For now, I'll walk in it, knowing it's what makes my future. The tears, the hope, the laughter, the anguish. It's for my future.

I wouldn't give it up for anything.

Acknowledgments

Every time I look back at my work, the clear truth hits me like a sack of potatoes. Really heavy, but also really good because potatoes are amazing gifts that should be cherished. Never underestimate how far a few potatoes can go. But I digress.

The truth is that I would never have gotten this far without the help and support of the following people.

First and foremost, thank you to all my betas. Thank you to Kerri Beckman and her mom, who both spent a lot of time going through my manuscript and commenting on the material, and also introducing me to the world of writers. Thank you to Daniel Burkeen, who also took the time to read the early drafts of my novel and give me feedback. Thank you to Jacki Salazar, who supported me and read the book in its very early stages. Thank you to Gay Crissman Clark for always believing in my work and also reading the book. Thank you to my grandma, Jennye Giles, and my aunt, Jill Giles, for reading through my book and continuing to support it. Thank you to Zarina Anito who, despite having a busy student schedule, took the time to read my early works and give me a list with feedback (the longer the giraffe, the higher it is). And lastly, thank you to Adriana Bolanos for being so enthusiastic about my book and also giving me feedback on the first drafts. You guys were some of the first people to join me on this journey, and I couldn't have done it without you.

Thank you to my friends and family for always supporting me. My grandparents, my relatives, and my close friends who were very eager to read my book, thank you. Even if you weren't a beta, you still helped me pull through. It didn't matter that you hadn't read my book (and on some occasions, I evilly made you wait until the release) because you still believed in it until the very end. Thank you to all my teachers, especially all my writing teachers, for always encouraging me and planting a love for writing in me since day one.

Thank you to my cover artist, T.M. Franklin. I'm in love with the design you created, and the novel wouldn't have such an awesome flair without you.

A huge thank you to my editor, Linda Hill. Your work and effort helped me bring out the best in my story, and I definitely wouldn't be where I am without you. You're kind, and not fooling around with your comments and feedback, yet you still manage to make me chuckle and smile. And though I've never had any other editors, I know I wouldn't trade you out for anyone else.

A special thanks to Rainne Mendoza Celespara for your help in walking us through this. You helped my mom with the business portion of my book, and you gave me some really helpful tips, one author to another. Without you, we'd never know how to get this book out there. You helped in guiding us and showing us the ropes when it came to publishing, and I just can't thank you enough for jumping at the chance to help me out.

The biggest thanks to my parents, Lilibeth and Wade Giles. Man, I'm not sure what I'd do without you guys. I mean, I wouldn't even be alive without you. Thank you to my mom who organized everything for me and pushed me to keep going even when I didn't feel like it. I may have written the book, but you're the one who brought it to life. You turned my idea into a reality. Thank you to my dad who paid for a lot of this (who knew writing a book could be so expensive?), and who never pushed away the idea that I could be a writer. You brought light into my days with your humor and your knowledge of words and grammar. You both encouraged me to follow my dreams, and I can't thank you enough for all you've done. Thank you both so much for your faith in me. I love you guys.

And my greatest and endless gratitude be to God, who stayed by my side every step of the way. He blessed me with this opportunity, and I'm so, so, so grateful for all He's done.

About the Author

Casey Giles is a teenage author who lives in the fourth largest city in North America with her family and hyper-active dog, Boodle. She enjoys fine arts and history, plays the violin, and does digital art and animation. INDIFFERENTS was inspired by her love of reading and writing.

This is her first novel.

Connect with Casey at:
Email: boodledoodle11@gmail.com
Instagram: @kaesse_
Facebook: @CaseyAuthorIndifferents

Made in the USA
Coppell, TX
28 December 2019